# GOAL LINE

# GOAL LINE

Tiki Barber and Ronde Barber
with Paul Mantell

A Paula Wiseman Book
Simon & Schuster Books for Young Readers
New York  London  Toronto  Sydney

For AJ, Chason, Riley, and Ella—T. B.

For my three roses—R. B.

SIMON & SCHUSTER BOOKS FOR YOUNG READERS
An imprint of Simon & Schuster Children's Publishing Division
1230 Avenue of the Americas, New York, New York 10020
This book is a work of fiction. Any references to historical events, real people, or real locales
are used fictitiously. Other names, characters, places, and incidents are products of the
authors' imagination, and any resemblance to actual events or locales or persons, living or
dead, is entirely coincidental.
SIMON & SCHUSTER BOOKS FOR YOUNG READERS is a trademark of Simon & Schuster, Inc.
For information about special discounts for bulk purchases, please contact Simon & Schuster
Special Sales at 1-866-506-1949 or business@simonandschuster.com.
The Simon & Schuster Speakers Bureau can bring authors to your live event. For more
information or to book an event, contact the Simon & Schuster Speakers Bureau
at 1-866-248-3049 or visit our website at www.simonspeakers.com.
Book design by Krista Vossen
The text for this book is set in Melior.
Manufactured in the United States of America
0711 FFG
Library of Congress Cataloging-in-Publication Data
Barber, Tiki, 1975–
Goal line / Tiki Barber and Ronde Barber with Paul Mantell.—1st ed.
p. cm.
"A Paula Wiseman Book."
Summary: When identical twin brothers Ronde and Tiki Barber grow at different rates the
summer before their last year at Hidden Valley Junior High, their relationship both on and off
the football field changes.
ISBN 978-1-4169-9095-6 (hardcover)
ISBN 978-1-4424-3124-9 (eBook)
[1. Barber, Tiki, 1975– —Fiction. 2. Barber, Ronde, 1975– —Fiction. 3. Twins—Fiction.
4. Brothers—Fiction. 5. Growth—Fiction. 6. Football—Fiction.] I. Barber, Ronde, 1975–
II. Mantell, Paul. III. Title.
PZ7.B23328Gog 2011
[Fic]—dc23
2011013222

FIRST
EDITION

## ACKNOWLEDGMENTS

The authors and publisher gratefully
acknowledge Mark Lepselter for his help in making this book.

# EAGLES' ROSTER
## 9TH GRADE HIDDEN VALLEY JUNIOR HIGH SCHOOL

HEAD COACH—SAM WHEELER
DEFENSIVE COACH—PETE PELLUGI
OFFENSIVE COACH—STEVE ONTKOS

**QB**
MANNY ALVARO, GRADE 8
JONAH JAMES, GRADE 8

**WR**
FRANK AMADOU, GRADE 7
FELIX AMADOU, GRADE 7

**RB**
TIKI BARBER, GRADE 9
LUKE FRAZIER, GRADE 8

**CB**
RONDE BARBER, GRADE 9
JUSTIN LANDZBERG, GRADE 8

**TE**
HAYDEN BROOK, GRADE 7

**S**
ALISTER EDWARDS, GRADE 8

**OL**
PACO RIVERA, (C), GRADE 9

**K**
ADAM COSTA, GRADE 9

**DL**
ROB FIORILLA, GRADE 7

**SPECIAL TEAMS**
RIO IKEDA, GRADE 7

## CONFERENCE SCHEDULE

EAST SIDE MOUNTAINEERS
NORTH SIDE ROCKETS
BLUE RIDGE BEARS
PULASKI WILDCATS
JEFFERSON PANTHERS
MARTINSVILLE COLTS
WILLIAM BYRD BADGERS
PATRICK HENRY PATRIOTS
MARTINSVILLE COLTS
NORTH SIDE ROCKETS
BLUE RIDGE BEARS
PULASKI WILDCATS

# CHAPTER ONE

## A "LITTLE" PROBLEM

*"I'M OPEN, TIKI!"*

Ronde Barber threw his hands up into the air as he ran. Way back down the street his twin brother hauled off and threw a perfect spiral, high and long. Ronde, in full stride, reached out to grab it. He could feel his fingertips brush the ball—

*HOONNNKKK!!!*

The car horn made Ronde wince, pull his hands in, and dodge to the left, all in the same instant. Ronde leaned against Mr. Evans's parked Oldsmobile, while the speeding car swerved to avoid the bouncing football, then continued on down the block, its horn blaring.

The driver yelled something out the window about ". . . kids! Playing in the middle of the street!" But Ronde couldn't make it out, and he didn't care to. He knew it was nothing he wanted to hear.

"Man!" he said breathlessly as he retrieved the ball, then trotted back to where Tiki was standing, shaking his head. "Why'd you throw the ball, dude? Didn't you see him coming?"

1

Tiki shook his head. "That guy was bustin' it! He wasn't even *there* when I let it loose."

"He must think this is the highway," said Ronde. Amherst Street was a dead end, and kids were always playing in the middle of the road. That was one of the great things about living here, in his opinion. Cars came by only every ten minutes or so.

"Come on," Tiki said. "Let's play that down over."

The twins were in the middle of one of their favorite pastimes—a kind of fantasy football that was the perfect way to spend a late summer afternoon. It had been eight whole months since they'd played in a real football game. *Eight months!* Every year by the end of August they were totally football-crazy.

Luckily, today was Labor Day—only a few days until *real* football started back at Hidden Valley Junior High!

"I would have had that ball, easy," Ronde pointed out as they walked back to the manhole cover that served as the line of scrimmage. "Stupid cars."

"Man, I can't wait till we're playing again for *real*."

Ronde had to laugh. "I never thought I'd see the day when we couldn't wait for school to start."

The next day school would be back in session, and they would be ninth graders at last—not to mention that they'd be team co-captains of the Hidden Valley Eagles, reigning champions of the entire state of Virginia!

"This year's going to be awesome," Tiki said. "Our last year, and we're gonna go out with a bang!"

"A *big* bang," Ronde said, a huge smile on his face. "Can you say 'all-star'?"

"Can you say 'two-time state champs'?"

"Can you say 'undefeated'?"

"Can you say 'record books'?"

"Uh-huh."

"Uh-huh."

They exchanged their special handshake—not the one everybody on the team used to celebrate big moments, but the one known to just the two of them, that they brought out only for very special occasions.

"Can you say 'NFL'?" Ronde said, voicing their deepest wish, the one they both dreamed about at night.

"The only thing is," Tiki said, his smile fading, "every kid in school is *expecting* us to do all that."

"So?"

"So, you know it's not gonna be easy. What if we . . ." He swallowed hard. "You know . . ."

"Don't talk like that!" Ronde told him. "You know what Mom would say."

"And Coach, too," Tiki said.

"Stay positive!"

Ronde and Tiki understood that once you let negative thoughts into your brain, they made themselves at home, took over the place—and all of a sudden, your confidence was gone, and so was your game!

"Okay, same play again," Tiki said, clapping his twin on the back. "Third and ten, right?"

"Right."

Ronde loved these sessions of theirs—no pressure, and you could let your imagination go wild. In real life he played cornerback and kick returner. But here in the street he could be a wide receiver, or a running back like Tiki, or even quarterback if he felt like it. It was a real summer luxury. Starting tomorrow it would be back to school, and the team, and the Barber boys would be all business.

"Hut! Hut!" Tiki shouted. Ronde took off at full speed. He made one killer move, then another, and whooshed down the side of the street, alongside the parked cars. The ball met him in full stride—

*HONNNKKK!!*

"Not again," Ronde moaned, flattening himself into the side of a parked car to let the new intruder pass. But then he saw that it was their mom, driving the old brown station wagon.

She rolled down the window and pulled up beside him. "Can't you see when there's a car coming, Ronde?"

"Sure I can!" he said. "I knew you were there, Ma."

She frowned. "You've got to keep a better eye out than that," she said, "or I'm going to have to put my foot down."

"Yes, Mom," Ronde said.

"Now come on home," she said. "I've got a pile of new clothes for you and your brother to try on."

She continued on down the street and pulled into their driveway, while Ronde trotted after her, tossing the football to himself as he went.

Ronde hated trying stuff on, and he wished his mom would let him and Tiki pick out their own clothes. But Mrs. Barber was very strict about certain things. Every year she waited for the Labor Day sales, then spent the day hitting all the stores, looking for bargains.

"I don't intend to pay extra money just so you boys can dress in the latest styles that'll be old-fashioned the day after tomorrow," she would say.

The clothes she picked out were always well made, so they would last a long time. Mrs. Barber worked hard at two jobs, and she knew that money didn't grow on trees.

Ronde and Tiki helped her take the bags inside. Then the free-for-all began, both boys grabbing whatever items caught their eye, trying to get their pick before the other one claimed it.

"Don't fight over them!" Mrs. Barber ordered. "There's plenty for both of you. I got two of everything too, just in case you've grown a size. Whatever doesn't fit, I'll just return tomorrow."

Ronde gathered his choices in both arms and headed up to their bedroom. There he started trying on jeans, shirts, pants, and sweaters.

Tiki was over by his bed, doing the same thing.

"How do these look?" Ronde asked, showing Tiki the brown corduroy pants he was wearing.

Tiki shrugged. "Not too bad."

"Great," Ronde murmured. "At least you didn't laugh."

"Ha!"

"Funny," said Ronde, getting ready to try on another pair. "Very funny."

"Hey," Tiki said suddenly, looking down at his legs. "These pants are too small for me."

"Too *small*?" Ronde repeated. "Didn't Mom say she got a size larger, just in case?"

"Well, not these," Tiki said, taking them off. "See for yourself."

Ronde eyed the pair of pants. They were gray, and he kind of liked them. Of course, if they were small for Tiki, they were sure to be small for him, too. After all, they were identical twins. Until junior high they'd shared all their clothes.

To Ronde's surprise and shock, the pants fit him perfectly. He whipped them back off as fast as he could, hoping Tiki hadn't noticed.

No such luck. Tiki's eyes were bugging out, and he wore a big grin. "Hey," he said, "stand next to me, Ronde."

"Why?"

"Just come on over here by me," Tiki said, pointing to the floor at his feet, "and let's stand back-to-back."

"What for?"

"What do you think?" Tiki said, pointing again. "I bet you I'm taller than you."

"Can't be."

"Come on. Let's just see. What are you, chicken?"

Seeing that there was no way out, Ronde sighed and stood back-to-back with his brother in front of the mirror.

"Look at that!" Tiki crowed. "I'm at least *three inches* taller than you!"

"Three inches? No way!" Ronde protested. "Maybe one inch at most."

"*Three*, my man. One, two, three. Maybe even *four*!"

"Wait a second," Ronde said. "Something's wrong with this picture. Maybe I'm just all scrunched up." He went over to the chinning bar that was set into the door-way of their room, and hung from it for a few seconds. "Now try again," he told Tiki.

But he hadn't stretched out at all. Tiki was right. He was at least three inches taller than Ronde.

Tiki looked him up and down. "You look skinny, too, next to me," he commented. Making a muscle, he said, "Come on, let's see yours."

Ronde rolled up his sleeve and matched biceps with Tiki. "They're the exact same."

"No way! Come on, now. You're not blind. I'm taller than you, *and* I've got bigger muscles."

Ronde opened his mouth to say something, but he

7

couldn't for the life of him think of a single word. His head was pounding, and the whole room was starting to spin. He sat down on the bed and put his head into his hands.

This was a major *disaster*!

"Come on over to the scale," said Tiki, grabbing Ronde's arm and dragging him to the bathroom. "Here— look at that. I gained fifteen pounds!" He stepped off and said, "Your turn."

Sighing miserably, Ronde stepped onto the scale. The needle stopped at 82, the same exact weight he'd been at the beginning of the summer!

"Hey, Mom!" Tiki yelled.

"Shush!" Ronde told him, but it was too late. Their mother was already coming up the stairs.

"Mom, guess what! I'm bigger than Ronde!"

"Not by much," Ronde said through gritted teeth.

"Much, *much* bigger!" Tiki went on. "Look. Look at this," he said, dragging their mom into the bedroom. He tried on a shirt, showing her that the sleeves didn't come all the way to his wrists. "I'll bet this fits Ronde perfectly!"

"AAARRRGH!!!" With a roar Ronde leapt at Tiki, forcing him down onto the bed. Grabbing a pillow, he slammed his twin with it, over and over again.

Far from stopping Tiki, this just egged him on. Between gasps of laughter, Tiki said, "Don't be mad, Shorty. I can't help it if you didn't grow all summer! Ow! Ha, ha, ha! Ow!"

"Cut it out, Tiki!" Ronde shouted, slamming him once more with the pillow, then letting go of it to grab Tiki's arms and pin them to the bed.

"Stop it! Stop it, both of you!" Mrs. Barber demanded.

In an instant it was over. When their mom got that tone in her voice, they both froze in their tracks. "Now let me see what all this fuss is about."

She stood them back-to-back, and Ronde could see the surprise and concern in her face. "That's strange," she said. "Well, Ronde, I guess you'll be hitting your growth spurt any day now."

Seeing the tears he was fighting back, she went on. "Don't worry, baby. In the end you're both going to be the same exact size. That's the way it is with identical twins. It looks like your brother just got himself a little head start."

"It's not fair!" Ronde protested. "Why couldn't *I* have been the one to grow first?"

"Because I'm better than you," Tiki teased, drawing a little punch in the arm from Ronde. "Ow! Ha, ha, ha!"

"Tiki Barber, do not let me catch you making fun of your brother again!"

"No, Mom," said Tiki, his smile vanishing.

"Your job is to stick up for him, especially if somebody *else* makes fun of him. But whatever happens, don't let it be *you* doing the teasing."

"No, Mom."

9

"Now finish up with these clothes," she said. "We've still got to go buy school supplies for tomorrow."

After she left, Ronde went back over to his own pile of clothes. But he still felt angry, and cheated. "You'd better not even mention it tomorrow," he warned his brother.

"All right, all right."

That was the last they spoke about it. But several times that evening Ronde caught sight of his brother checking himself out in the mirror, making muscles and standing up as straight as he could.

That made the sting come right back, full strength. Suddenly Ronde wasn't looking forward to school—not in the least.

Sure enough, his troubles began before the boys even got to school. On the bus that morning their friend Paco Rivera, who played center for the Eagles and who had known the twins since they were little kids, got onto the bus and sat right behind them.

It was the first time they'd seen Paco since June, when he'd gone off to Mexico with his parents for the summer, to see his grandparents and cousins in the old country.

Paco greeted them excitedly in the aisle, and the twins rose to greet him, giving him the team handshake. Then Paco suddenly stopped, squinted, and tilted his head to one side. "Is it just me," he asked, "or is one of you guys bigger than the other?"

Tiki opened his mouth to speak, but Ronde squeezed his arm before he could get a word out. "Ow!" Tiki cried. "Quit it, Ronde!"

"So, Tiki," Paco said, breaking out into a grin, "you're the big Barber now, huh? Slap me five, jumbo!"

Tiki smiled back at him, and they high-fived with gusto. Then Paco turned to Ronde. "Tough break, little dude," he said. "But hey, don't worry. Cornerbacks don't have to be tall."

"Don't be a jerk, Paco," Ronde muttered.

"Why? What'd I say?"

"Tiki and I are gonna grow up to be the same exact size."

"Yeah, but *look* at him, dude. He's gonna be a monster at running back this year! We're gonna rule, you guys!"

"Yeah! That's what I'm talkin' about!" Tiki said, nodding. The two of them high-fived a second time.

Tiki had made a promise to their mom not to say anything, and he was as good as his word. But *Paco* hadn't made any promises. Within two minutes every kid on the bus knew about Ronde's "little" predicament—and as soon as they got off, they'd be sure to tell all their friends. Before long "Shorty" would be the talk of the entire school!

Ronde just sat there shaking his head as the others piled off the bus. Was it going to be like this all year long?

He finally dragged himself off the seat and out of the

bus. He trudged up the steps to the school as if his book bag weighed a ton. He tried not to walk too close to Tiki, so kids couldn't tell the difference in size between them. But he still felt their eyes on him.

Since he didn't look back at them, he couldn't tell whether they were eyeing him with admiration—the star of the Eagles' defense—or whether they were comparing him to his brother, and laughing to themselves as they noticed how small he was in comparison.

Luckily, things were not so bad once the bell rang and homeroom started. No one was looking at Ronde now. They were all busy comparing program cards, catching up with friends they hadn't seen all summer, and, finally, shuffling off to their first class of the new school year.

Heading for Mr. Lerner's first-period science class, Ronde heaved a sigh of relief. Finally he could think about something other than his own shrimpiness!

## CHAPTER TWO

## BIG MAN ON CAMPUS

---

*"YO, TEE-KEEEE!!"*

"My main man!!"

"Woo-hoo, big dog! What have you been eating all summer?"

Tiki high-fived everybody who stuck their hand out as they passed him in the halls. He breathed deeply, drinking it all in. His smile stretched from ear to ear, and he nodded his head as if to say, *Yeah, this is really happening!*

Everybody knew him here, and they all wanted to claim him as their best friend. He was a big man on campus, and this year he was even *bigger*—four inches and twenty-five pounds bigger than last June, to be exact!

"How tall are you exactly?" Cootie Harris, the Eagles' number one fan, wanted to know. Cootie was the team mascot and unofficial good-luck charm. He wore a big feathery Eagle suit on the sidelines each game day, and flapped his wings whenever the team scored or made a big play on defense. He took a lot of teasing for his antics and his costume, but he always took it good-naturedly.

So Tiki was pleased to give him the extra attention he deserved.

"I'm five foot six and three quarters," Tiki said proudly. "And they say once you start your growth spurt, you never know how far it will go."

Those were comforting words for Cootie, Tiki knew. The poor little guy was probably less than five feet tall, and still hoping for that magical spurt to start. Tiki noticed that Cootie's voice was cracking when he got excited. "That's a good sign," Tiki told him. "It means you're gonna shoot up soon."

"Really? Wow, so cool!" said Cootie, practically flapping his wings as he bounced away down the hall.

Tiki laughed and shook his head. Then he thought of poor Ronde, and what he must have been going through that morning.

Then the bell rang for last period, and Tiki had to get to class. His English teacher was Ms. Adair. She was nice and cheerful, but also no-nonsense. No sooner did they all sit down than she started handing out a bunch of papers, and writing instructions on the board for all sorts of things.

It took him a long time, but Tiki wrote everything down. Just when he was done, and was sticking all the papers into his backpack, she started in again.

"Now, class," she began, "I'm happy to announce that Hidden Valley Junior High School will be participating in the President's National Essay Contest!"

She was wearing a big, happy smile, but the murmur that went around the classroom was anything but happy. Tiki knew why, too.

Half the kids didn't like writing, because they weren't good at it, or they thought it was boring, or it took too long when they would rather be doing something else. The other half just figured this essay contest boiled down to more work, on top of everything else all their teachers made them do.

It seemed to Tiki that every teacher thought that the only work you had to do was the work *they* gave you.

"The topic of the essay will be 'the true meaning of a famous American saying.' As you all know, we use famous sayings all the time, and almost never realize what they mean or how they came to be famous. This is your chance to explore the saying of your choice. That's why this contest is so exciting! You get to choose whatever saying you like."

Kathi Sienkiewicz raised her hand. "Ms. Adair?" she asked.

"Yes, Kathi?"

"What if we don't want to do it?"

Another murmur rose from the class. Tiki whistled low. Kathi sure had guts to ask a question like that—one they all wanted the answer to.

"The contest is mandatory, Kathi," said the teacher.

"Manda-what?"

15

"Manda-tory. It means you have to, dear. Every student at Hidden Valley will be writing an essay, and anyone can win!"

"Even seventh graders?" Kathi asked, not happy about it. Kathi was a ninth grader and felt that ought to give her special privileges.

"Anyone!" Ms. Adair said brightly. "Maybe even someone from this class! Wouldn't that be thrilling?"

Tiki rolled his eyes. He wondered whether "Oh, brother!" would qualify as a famous saying.

"You will have two weeks to write your essay, which should be no less than one thousand words. That's about five double-spaced pages."

"*Two weeks* to write a *thousand words*?" another student piped up.

"That's right," said Ms. Adair. "I know it's not much time, but Dr. Anand wants you all to improve your writing skills, and she knows we teachers don't give as much homework the first weeks."

A groan went up from the class. They all knew that no matter how little homework you got the first two weeks, it always felt like a lot, because you hadn't done any all summer. Now they'd all have to do this stupid essay on top of everything else!

The bell rang to signal the end of the school day. Tiki stuffed the essay announcement into his book bag with the rest of the papers and filed out of the room. He had no idea what he'd write about, but he could think about that later. Right now he had someplace more important to go—

Football practice!

Coach Wheeler took one look at Tiki and said, "*Whoa. Son, we're gonna have to get you another uniform—one in a larger size, for sure.*"

Tiki beamed, and so did Wheeler. They both knew what Tiki's larger size meant to the team. More power, more yards, more points, and more wins!

"Good to see you back, Tiki," said Wheeler, clapping him on the back. "Why don't you get out there and help with the rookies?"

Today was tryouts, and the new crop of seventh graders looked really good. Was it Tiki's imagination, or were they much bigger than seventh graders used to be, back when he was one?

What were they feeding kids these days? he wondered. Whatever it was, they must have been eating a *lot* of it. Even though he'd grown so much, most of these seventh graders were *still* bigger than he was!

Tiki and the regulars from last season all greeted one another, slapping five, making cracks, and horsing around. Then Coach Wheeler blew the whistle, and they lined up on offense, facing a defensive line of new, nervous-looking faces.

Tiki remembered what it had been like back when he

and Ronde had been trying out. Every play could make you or break you. If you messed up and a coach saw it, they'd give you a bad mark for that skill. And if you got enough bad marks, you didn't make the team.

Tiki took a handoff on the first play, and put a move on the defensive end that left him grabbing two handfuls of air.

"Hey, stay loose, yo," Tiki told the kid as he passed him on his way back to the huddle. "It's gonna be all right. Just play proud."

It was his mom's saying, and it had become his and Ronde's motto. He didn't know if the kid got the meaning of it, but Tiki was pretty sure he got the general idea.

The next time Tiki ran his way, the kid dove, grabbed him by the ankles, and brought him down.

"That's the way!" Tiki told him, helping the boy up. "What's your name?"

"Rob Fiorilla," the kid said, grinning shyly.

"Tiki Barber."

"Yeah, I know," said Rob.

Tiki chuckled. He still couldn't quite believe he was so famous that even seventh graders, new to the school, knew who he was.

"Did you see the play that kid just made?" Tiki asked as Ronde came jogging up to them.

"You're just slow today," he told Tiki, chuckling.

"This is my twin brother, Ronde," Tiki told Rob. "Ronde, meet Rob Fiorilla."

"Your *twin*?" Rob repeated, looking at one, then the other, and squinting his eyes. "How come you're so much bigger?"

Tiki could practically see the steam coming out of Ronde's ears. Luckily, Coach Pellugi called the defense away for drills and Ronde and Rob jogged off together, leaving Tiki and the offense behind.

Coach Ontkos gathered the other players and the would-be Eagles around. "Okay," he said. "Let's see how you kids can catch the ball."

Tiki spotted two tall skinny boys with long legs and arms. Amazingly, it seemed there might now be *two* sets of identical twins on the Eagles!

They lined up along with the others, then proceeded to run several patterns, with starting quarterback Manny Alvaro throwing to them. The tall, lanky twins each made spectacular grabs.

Their names were Felix and Frank Amadou. They had moved to Roanoke from Haiti last year, and English was still their second language. More important, they were at least three inches taller than Tiki, even now that he'd grown some.

Ronde, covering them, was giving up at least six inches. The Amadou brothers had long strides. They could jump, they had good hands, and they even busted a few choice moves Tiki thought might be worth using himself.

"Sign those two up!" Paco said in Tiki's ear.

"Ow!" Tiki said. "Hey, don't make me deaf, man!"

"Sorry. I'm just excited," said Paco.

"I hear that. I think we might have Sam Scarfone's spot covered too."

He meant the defensive end position, which Sam had starred at the past two years. Rob Fiorilla had a lot to learn, but he also had all the talent he'd need to stop a running back with Tiki's kind of skills.

Not only was the new crop of players looking exceptional, but all the returning Eagles were bigger, stronger, and more experienced. All except Ronde. Manny Alvaro in particular looked like he might turn into a real star this season. Yes, the Eagles' future was looking very bright this afternoon, Tiki thought.

But just then the sun hid itself behind a dark cloud. At the same instant a shout went up from the other side of the field, where the tryouts for defense were going on.

"Shut up!" The words rang out loud and clear. It was Ronde's voice!

"Make me!" came the reply. And now other boys were holding Ronde and his opponent apart. Whistles blew, and coaches came running.

Tiki ran too, as fast as his longer, stronger legs could carry him. If he had to defend his brother, he would. But it would be better to stop the fight before it got started.

By the time he got there, luckily, things had already

calmed down. The other boy had gone off to his next drill, along with most of the other kids. Ronde stood where he was, steaming, each of his arms held by one of his teammates.

"What's up, Ronde?" Tiki asked.

"Some punk seventh grader was messing with me."

"What does that mean?" Tiki pressed him.

Ronde stared off into the distance, where the offending kid was trying out at cornerback—Ronde's position. The kid was big, much taller than Ronde, and with longer legs. He seemed to have pretty good skills, too.

"Wow," Tiki said as the kid knocked away a pass that would have been a sure completion. "He's gonna be good. Look at the size of him!"

Then he realized what he'd said, just as Ronde's fist came crashing into his arm. "Sorry, dude. I forgot. Sorry. Sorry."

Still, Tiki thought, it was good that the Eagles would have another strong cornerback. It meant that other teams wouldn't be able to avoid Ronde by throwing to whichever receiver he wasn't covering.

The Eagles had lost a lot of their best players over the summer, but it sure looked like they were restocking with supertalented rookies. Tiki couldn't help feeling they had a real shot at repeating as state champs—*if* Ronde could get over being the smallest guy on the team.

Right now that looked like a great big *if*.

# CHAPTER THREE

## ANTICIPATION

**RONDE COULD FEEL THE RECEIVER'S EYES ON HIM.** He could see that sneering smile behind the face guard. He knew what the kid was thinking.

"I may be short," Ronde said to himself, "but I'm no pushover."

The receiver's smirk turned into a wide grin. "We'll see about that."

Huh? Had he heard Ronde's words? How could he have? Ronde had barely breathed them!

No time to think about that, though. The game was on! The quarterback took the snap, and the receiver came straight at Ronde!

Ronde braced himself for the hit. Usually it was him giving the hits, and the receiver taking them. Not this time.

This receiver was huge—a foot taller than Ronde, and at least fifty pounds heavier. Not only that, it was all muscle. Ronde swallowed hard and braced for impact.

But it didn't come. When he opened his eyes (had he really closed them?), the receiver was already past him, racing downfield, waving his hands and yelling, "I'm open! I'm open!"

The crowd was roaring in Ronde's ears, and somehow he heard every word they were saying. How had the guy gotten past him like that?

He tried desperately to make up the lost ground. But the receiver, with his long legs that took such long strides, had a huge head start.

Not only that, but Ronde suddenly felt like he was running through mud. His legs felt heavy, and the air felt like a thick soup he had to fight through. He looked up and saw the ball sailing over his head, just out of reach.

He frantically tried to bat it down, but it was too high. Everything was out of reach, in fact. The ball, the receiver, the goal line. No matter how fast he tried to run, they all remained out of reach.

Why? Why did he have to be so small? It was infuriating! The receiver had caught the pass now, and was crossing the goal line for a touchdown. Ronde grabbed his helmet with both hands and yelled, "NoooooOOOO!!!!"

Suddenly the earth was shaking. No, wait, it was him—someone was shaking him.

"Ronde!"

"Let go of me!" he cried. "I'm just too little. I can't play anymore! I quit!"

"Ronde! Dude, wake up!"

"Huh?" Ronde opened his eyes, and found himself staring at himself.

No. Wait. It was Tiki. Of course. He'd been dreaming!

"What . . . hey . . ."

"Snap out of it, dude. You were having a nightmare or something."

"Ha. I'll say," Ronde replied, breaking out into a relieved grin.

So it hadn't happened after all. He hadn't blown anything, or cost his team a touchdown or a game. The season hadn't even started.

But what would happen when it did? Would his nightmare come true?

"Ronde," said Tiki, "listen up. Just because you're not growing as fast as me, it doesn't mean you've lost your talent."

"What?" Ronde said, avoiding Tiki's eyes.

"You know what I'm talking about. It's not your talent you have to worry about, dude. It's your mojo."

"My mojo?"

"Your confidence. Don't stop believing in yourself, Ronde," Tiki said. "You're still the same guy you've always been."

"That's true," Ronde said. "Tiki . . . was I talking in my sleep?"

"Big-time."

"Dang."

"Remember what I said, now."

"I will. That's good advice. Thanks, Tiki."

"Don't mention it. Go back to sleep. And no more of those nightmares, okay?"

Almost a week had passed since the start of school. It was Friday, and that morning the new Eagles' team list had been posted in the hallway outside the main office.

Ronde passed the crowd of seventh graders huddling in front of it, looking for their names on the roster. Some kids were yelling "Yesss!" and others were sighing and turning away, disappointed.

Heading to his first class, Ronde remembered the feeling. It had been two years since he and Tiki had first been huddled in front of that list, along with their friends. But that was life. Sometimes you succeeded in reaching your goals, and sometimes you failed.

And once in a while you succeeded but still weren't happy. He and Tiki had made the team, all right, but then they'd had to spend most of that first season on the bench, watching the older kids play while they waited for a brief chance to get on the field and strut their stuff.

In English class Ms. Bernstein reminded them that by Monday they had to hand in their essay topics for approval. Ronde bit his lip. He'd forgotten all about the contest. He'd been so busy with football practice, schoolwork, reconnecting with friends, and worrying about his size, that he hadn't given the contest a moment's thought.

Now he'd have to come up with something fast.

All day long he listened for someone to use a popular saying he could steal for his essay. But no one did—or at least they didn't use any sayings he liked.

"A penny saved is a penny earned" wasn't too bad, but he couldn't see writing a thousand words about it. Besides, he figured lots of kids would use that one. "The early bird catches the worm" was a nonstarter. Ronde hated getting up early. It was all he could do to get himself out of bed in time to catch the school bus!

He was glad when the day finally ended and he could head down to the locker room to meet his new teammates.

The locker room was a beehive of activity, with everyone trying on their new practice jerseys and helmets. He went straight over to Tiki, who was in the center of a big group of veteran players.

"Hey, you guys!" Ronde greeted them. "What's up?"

"Ronde!" a few of them shouted, high-fiving him.

"Yo, little man!" Paco said, giving him a clap on the back.

Ronde gritted his teeth and tried not to let Paco's offhand remark get to him. He'd been "little man" to Paco and some of the other Eagles since seventh grade. And he knew it wouldn't stop, not until he got at least as big as Tiki was now.

Across the room the new players were busy getting

acquainted with one another. Ronde went over and said hello to some of them, starting with the tall, skinny twins who had obviously been tapped as the Eagles' wide receivers of the future. "Yo. Ronde Barber," he said, offering his hand.

"Felix Amadou," said one of the twins.

"Frank," said the other, and they both shook hands with Ronde.

"I see where you guys are gonna switch off starting," Ronde said. "That's way cool."

"Yeah," said Frank. "But I'm way better than Felix."

His twin gave him a playful punch in the arm. "He's just bragging," he said. "We both know I'm better."

Ronde laughed, wondering if all identical twins joked around the same way with each other. It was just like watching him and Tiki!

"See you out there," he told them. "But just to let you know, neither one of you is catching anything today. Not with me covering."

"Whoa!" they both said, grinning and nodding their heads. "Listen to him!"

"Just bustin' your chops," Ronde said, giving them both a slap on the back. "Good luck this year. We're gonna need you guys."

"Thanks, dude," said Felix.

"Yeah, thanks," said Frank. "Seriously."

Next Ronde went over to Rob Fiorilla, the kid Tiki had

introduced him to. "Hey," he said. "My brother thinks you're gonna be a big man on the defensive line."

"I hope so," said Rob, smiling bashfully. "Did he really say that about me?"

"Uh-huh. Don't stress yourself out, though," Ronde advised him. "There's a whole lot to learn. It takes time, so don't be too hard on yourself."

"Thanks," said Rob. "I appreciate the good word."

Coach Wheeler called the troops to order with an earsplitting toot of his whistle. Some kids laughed, covering their ears—including Ronde. That was just Coach's way. When he wanted your attention, he got it, no doubt.

"Okay. Welcome, Eagles! Welcome back, reigning state champions!" he began, to a thunderous cheer. "Welcome back to my boys, and welcome for the first time to my new guys! Let's give it up for the seventh graders!"

Another cheer followed, and then Coach Wheeler grew more serious. "Okay, troops. We're gonna go out and do some basic drills and have a little scrimmage. I want you to go as hard as you can without hurting yourselves. Remember, it takes a few practices to get in true game shape. But by next week we ought to be there, if we buckle down and work really hard.

"Today I want the starters on defense facing the subs on offense, and vice versa. That way you'll get the feel of working with the guys you'll be alongside all year. So let's get out there, take it one play at a time, and see what we've got going, okay?"

One last cheer from the team, and they were on their way out of the locker room, through the big double doors, and out onto the bright green of the Eagles' field. To Ronde it felt like home.

After an hour of routine drills—because of the two-month break, the drills were supertiring—Ronde's group of defenders lined up on the thirty-five yard line against an offense made up of seventh and eighth graders. The eighth graders hadn't seen much action last year, and were excited that now they'd be a real part of the mix.

The seventh graders had been totally wiped out by the series of unfamiliar, intense drills. Tomorrow, Ronde knew, they'd be sore all over. So would they all, for that matter. Still, the newbies were so psyched to be on the team that they kept jumping up and down in the huddle.

Ronde knew what they were feeling—he'd been in their shoes, after all—but after two years on the Eagles, he had learned not to waste an ounce of his precious energy. A seasoned veteran now, he approached his work calmly, saving his energy for the actual plays on the field.

He lined up opposite Felix Amadou. Lifting his helmet, Ronde gave him a wink and said, "Bring it on, dude."

"You asked for it, little guy," Felix shot back, teasing.

While Ronde steamed, Felix clapped his hands twice and then got into his set as Jonah James, an eighth grader who would be the team's second-string quarterback, called the signals behind center. "Hut! Hut, hut! Hut!"

On the snap, Felix took off at full gallop. Ronde was much shorter, but he knew he could match anybody's speed, no matter how long their legs were. Not even trying to give Felix a bump, he kept up with him stride for stride. When the ball arrived, Ronde still had enough energy to make a final leap and knock it away.

"Nice going," Felix said, offering his hand.

Ronde gave Felix the team handshake. "Thanks. And don't call me 'little guy.'" Without waiting for a reply, he jogged back to the defensive huddle, leaving Felix to think it over.

Ronde looked over and saw Tiki and the starting offense lined up at the other thirty-five yard line, facing the second-string defenders in their own scrimmage. Manny Alvaro, the starting quarterback, took the snap but had to scramble as Rob Fiorilla raced around the end and came straight at him.

Darting to his weak side, Manny scrambled desperately, and ten yards downfield Tiki, seeing his QB in trouble, ran parallel to Manny so he could dump the ball to Tiki on the rollout.

The play wound up with a big gain, and Ronde was impressed by both sides—Fiorilla on defense (he'd completely fooled the starting right tackle), and Manny and Tiki on offense.

Those two seemed to have great chemistry together. Last year, with Cody Hansen at QB, there had been some problems, although the team had won the championship anyway. A scrambling quarterback like Manny was a perfect match for Tiki, with his quick run-and-cut style. "Those two are gonna tear it up!" Ronde said to himself.

Lining up again, he found himself covering Felix's twin, Frank. Ronde would never have known except that their numbers were different. Felix wore 89, Fred Soule's number from last season. Frank wore Joey Gallagher's old number, 88.

Once again Ronde played his man to perfection.

"Wow!" said Frank after Ronde deprived him of a sure touchdown. "You sure can play, for a little guy."

Ronde nodded his head. "That's right, big fella. Like I told your brother, don't call me 'little guy.' Just remember— good things come in small packages."

And then it hit him—the contest! He'd just come up with the perfect saying for his essay.

"So, what do you think?" Ronde asked Tiki and his mom as they sat together at dinner that night.

"'Good things come in small packages'?" Tiki said with a crooked grin. "I guess you might as well go with it."

"Tiki Barber," said their mom sharply, "are you teasing your brother?"

"No, Mom!" Tiki said quickly. "I—I was just saying I like his topic."

"And what is *your* topic going to be?" she pressed him.

Tiki shrugged. "I haven't got a clue, to tell you the truth. I'm totally stuck."

"Don't give up," Mrs. Barber told him. "You'll think of something, I'm sure."

"I'm sure I'm going to get an F," Tiki muttered.

"What? What did you just say?" their mom demanded.

"N-nothing, Mom."

"I heard you, young man. Now, don't you go giving up on yourself. I won't stand for it, and neither should you."

"Yes, Mom," Tiki said, looking down at his plate.

But she wasn't done with him yet. "Your brother couldn't think of anything either—until he *did*," she pointed out. "And you will too. Keep trying, never give up, and you'll find the perfect saying for you."

She patted him on the arm, then went into the living room to get something. While she was gone, Tiki muttered, "The perfect saying for me . . . Well, I guess I could say 'Good things come in *big* packages.'"

"I'm gonna tell Mom you said that."

"Don't you do it," Tiki warned.

"Tell me what?" said Mrs. B., coming back into the kitchen.

"Nothing," Ronde said. "We were just goofing around."

"Yeah," Tiki said, glad Ronde was willing to let it slide.

"Tiki," said their mom, "if this problem was about football, you know you'd find a solution."

"I guess that's true," Tiki admitted.

"Well, school is just as important. You're a good writer. You have nothing to be afraid of. Just bring the same attitude you bring to the football field."

"Yeah," Ronde said. "Play proud, Bro."

Tiki's eyes went wide. "That's it!" he cried, jumping out of his chair. "'Play proud!' That's my saying!"

"Wait a minute," Ronde said. "That's not a famous saying!"

"It is in *this* house," Tiki shot back.

Mrs. Barber settled it for them. "Well, if it's not famous, it ought to be. It was good enough to win the Eagles a championship, wasn't it? You go ahead and use 'Play proud,' Tiki. Maybe you'll be the one to make your mother's saying famous!"

# CHAPTER FOUR

## GAME ON!

*WHEN GAME DAY FINALLY ARRIVED, TIKI WAS* practically beside himself with excitement. He could barely wait to get into his uniform and out onto the field. For the team's opener Hidden Valley Junior High had gone all out to salute their champions.

The school band was in the bleachers, along with the cheerleaders down in front and the team mascot, Cootie, whipping everybody into a happy frenzy with his antics in his Eagle suit.

When the Eagles themselves ran onto the field, the drum corps struck up a thunderous beat, and the crowd yelled so loudly you couldn't hear yourself think. Glancing across the field at the East Side Mountaineers, Tiki felt sorry for them. The game hadn't even started, but they already looked beaten.

Last year the two teams had played a close game, with the Eagles coming out on top, 18–15. But that didn't tell the whole story. During that game Tiki had played not only running back, but also kicker, replacing Adam Costa, who had been suspended for flunking two of his courses.

This year both teams had a lot of new players. But it seemed to Tiki, just looking at the two teams, that the Eagles had gotten bigger and stronger, while the Mountaineers had lost most of their huge defensive linemen.

After a long, loud salute to the state champions, with Cootie running around the field holding their trophy from last season high over his head, the game finally began.

On the kickoff Ronde sped down the field in a blur and rammed into the Mountaineer return man so hard the kid nearly lost the ball.

The Mountaineers offense got to work, but they didn't get very far. Their quarterback seemed flustered, throwing behind his receivers twice, and getting sacked for a big loss on third down.

East Side punted, and Ronde's return put the ball at midfield. Tiki raced onto the field, eager to get to work. Coach Wheeler had sent his offense in with the first three plays already called, and the first one was an off-tackle play, featuring Tiki.

He took the ball from Manny and ran straight through a hole in the line created by the left guard and tackle.

Tiki felt a rush of excitement carrying him along. It was like he had kicked his playing into a higher gear and everyone around him was moving in slow motion. Putting on a dazzling move, he faked the linebacker right off his feet, and was into the open, heading straight for pay dirt!

He felt something grab his ankle at the ten yard line, and down he went, holding the ball tightly so it wouldn't come loose. The whistle blew, and he got up smiling. First and goal, Eagles, at the Mountaineers eight yard line!

The next play was a quick out pass to Frank Amadou, who was starting at wide receiver on the right side. He leapt and caught the ball high in the air, but came down out of bounds.

Tiki winced, a rookie mistake. But the kid would learn. He and his twin brother already had great skills; they just needed good coaching. And with the Eagles, they'd be sure to get just that.

On third down Coach Wheeler had called for a quick dump pass to Tiki in the flat. But they were in the red zone now, and the middle of the field would be crowded with defenders. So Wheeler sent the fullback, Luke Frazier, in with a different play—a handoff to Tiki right up the middle.

Tiki took the ball and headed straight for Paco. The beefy center was a true wide-body, and strong, too. He simply pushed the East Side nose tackle straight backward, and Tiki followed right behind.

After a slight fake to the left, Tiki darted right, catching the linebackers off guard. Before they could recover, he cut left again. With a last, desperate lunge, he leapt across the goal line and into the end zone!

It was the Eagles' first score of the year. Tiki roared and jumped for joy, spiking the ball as hard as he could. His teammates raced to his side, and they all hugged and danced around, so much so that the referee blew his whistle and called a penalty on them for excessive celebration!

When they got back to the sidelines, Coach Wheeler was furious. "You guys just cost us fifteen yards!" he barked. "Use your heads, will you?"

Tiki knew Coach was right. There was no point in rubbing the other team's noses in it. It only made them mad, and got them to play harder. The smart thing to do was just keep playing your game and let the fans do the celebrating for you.

Still, there was no arguing that the first score of the season was a big one. It set the stage for lots more. And the fact that Tiki was the one who'd scored seemed to announce that this year he would shine as the team's biggest, brightest star.

The second quarter started with the score 7–0, Eagles, but the Mountaineers were driving into field goal range. Tiki watched as Ronde covered East Side's best receiver like a blanket.

But the Mountaineers had learned from last year. They knew all about Ronde, and when they passed, it was always to the side of the field where he *wasn't*.

The Eagles' other starting corner, Justin Landzberg, was an eighth grader who hadn't seen much action last season. Though taller than Ronde, he wasn't nearly as fast, or as quick reacting to the other guys' moves. The Mountaineers now took advantage of that, scoring a touchdown of their own with a long bomb over Justin's head.

Now the game was tied, and it stayed that way until late in the quarter, when Ronde ran a Mountaineer punt all the way back to the East Side twenty-five. Then it was Tiki's turn to take over.

Since the Eagles' wide receivers were inexperienced— and in the case of the Amadou twins, rookies—Coach Wheeler had geared the Eagles offense toward the run and short pass—both of which featured Manny and Tiki.

Manny hadn't been a starter very much in the previous season, but he'd had enough experience to learn a lot. Besides, he was a talented natural athlete. Twice, breakdowns on the offensive line let blitzing pass rushers through. But Manny managed to dodge them long enough to find Tiki in the flat or at the sideline, or else he managed to run circles around the defenders until he turned a potential sack into a decent gain.

Now Manny's scrambling ability and Tiki's savvy and smarts combined to punish the Mountaineers. Once again the blitz got through the Eagles' line. Once more,

Manny avoided the first hit, then the second. He faked out a third blitzer by pretending to launch a long bomb, then ducked and darted to his right, looking for Tiki.

Tiki had gone out on a short pattern, which was partly why the blitz had gotten through. He hadn't been there to block them. Now, seeing that Manny was in trouble, he doubled back, giving his quarterback a target at the ten yard line. Manny spotted him, and threw a strike right to Tiki's chest.

The safety got to him almost immediately. Last season Tiki would've been dragged to the turf. But not this year. He was bigger and stronger, and he just kept himself upright, trudging foot after foot toward the end zone, dragging the safety on his back, then the other safety around his ankles, until he finally collapsed under the weight of three East Side defenders—at the one yard line!

On the next play Luke slammed it in for the touchdown. He, too, had grown over the summer and was now a perfect size for a fullback—big, muscular, and bulky. John Berra had been like that, and Tiki knew he was lucky to have another great blocker to work with this year.

The gun sounded the end of the first half with the Eagles on top, 14–7. In the locker room Coach Wheeler pumped them up. "Come on, you guys!" he yelled. "You should be up by twenty, not seven! You think those guys are just gonna lie down for you? You beat them last year by three points! Three!"

By the end of his speech, the Eagles were angry. They took that anger back out onto the field with them, and immediately took over the game. Ronde began the rout with a kickoff return for a touchdown.

"Woo-hoo!" he shouted as he ran back to the sideline. "Give it up for the little guy! I *told* you good things come in small packages!"

Tiki had to laugh. Ronde had gone from being insulted about it to using it as fuel to stoke his game. "Proud of you, Bro," he told Ronde.

"That's right, that's right," said Ronde, nodding and flashing a big smile.

By the end of the third quarter, the Eagles led by a score of 35–10, thanks to two eighty-yard drives featuring Tiki and Luke. The two of them took turns pounding out yards, showing no mercy to the tired Mountaineer defense, who had been on the field for most of the game and were clearly wilting in the heat.

The fourth quarter was almost scoreless, with the Eagles finally running out of energy themselves, but in the last two minutes the Mountaineers ran off ten straight points to make the final score a respectable 35–17, but it really wasn't as close as that.

The party went on long after the game, the Eagles' field swarming with fans dancing, barbecuing, and singing the team song. As soon as they'd changed into street clothes, Tiki, Ronde, and the rest of the Eagles came out to join the fun. They were in a great mood, and it showed in the way they talked.

"Oh, yeah," said Paco, jiggling his big body to the beat of the school band as they played a salsa number. "We are goin' . . . un-de-fea-ted . . . nhh . . . nhh-nhh . . . oh, yeah . . ."

Tiki laughed. "Take it easy, yo," he said. "It's only one game."

"Oh, yeah," Paco sang, nodding happily at Tiki. "And we win, we win . . ."

Tiki knew how he felt. It *was* only one game, but the easy victory sure felt a whole lot better than last year's opening loss. In fact, they'd spent that whole season trying to dig out of the hole they'd dug themselves by losing their first two games to lesser teams.

This year looked to be completely different. They'd beaten the lowly Mountaineers, just as expected. He and Manny had a great feel for each other's game. Luke had become a true bruiser, and the rookie class was looking like a bunch of future all-stars.

"You know, Paco," Tiki said, "I don't want to jinx anything, but I can really see us going undefeated."

"Oh, yeah," Paco sang in reply. "Oh-oh-oh-yeahhhh!!"

Just then Ronde came up to them. Tiki was dancing along with the others now. But Ronde wasn't.

"Cheer up, Shorty!" Paco told him. "You look like we lost the game."

Ronde shook his head. "No, man, but we could've. We didn't play like we should. At least not in the fourth quarter."

"Aw, come on, Ronde," Tiki said. "Paco's right. Let's celebrate, at least for today."

"Those guys were easy," Ronde pointed out. "We've got much tougher fish to fry starting next week. If we play like this against the Rockets, we're gonna lose. And that's no lie."

Tiki stopped jiggling, and even Paco slowed it down a little. "You are a downer, man," he told Ronde. "Why don't you just chill?"

"I'll celebrate when the season's over and we're the undefeated champs," Ronde replied. "And that's the way we all should play it."

"Aw, man," Paco said, frowning.

"No, he's right, Paco," Tiki said, putting a hand on the big guy's shoulder. "Let's not get ahead of ourselves."

"That's what I'm saying," Ronde agreed. "We've got to keep our minds sharp and focused. We haven't won anything yet, except a game we were supposed to win. We've got a lot of football still, and we need to win one game at a time."

At lunch in the cafeteria on Monday, Paco was out sick— too many hot dogs had given him a stomach problem— but all the other guys from the team were at their usual long table, kidding around with one another and talking about how great the team was.

"We're gonna stomp this whole league," said Justin.

"It's already over, baby," Luke agreed.

"Done deal," Manny chimed in.

"Hey. Guys," Tiki interrupted them. "Cut out the baloney."

"Huh?" They all looked at him, puzzled.

"You shouldn't be talkin' trash like that," he said. "It's dangerous."

Tiki told them what Ronde had said about not getting ahead of themselves—about staying focused, not taking anything for granted, playing one game at a time. He could see how they listened to him, with respect and admiration, as if he were their coach, not just another player. That's what it meant to be the team captain.

Yes, he told them everything Ronde had said, except he didn't tell them that it was Ronde who'd said it first.

Ronde wasn't there. He'd stayed late in study hall to finish writing his essay, which was due the next morning. Had he heard Tiki's words, he surely would have taken credit for them.

Now he came in, and after getting his food, he sat down across from Tiki, shoving himself into a tight space between Justin and Manny.

"What's up, guys?" he asked.

Tiki felt the blood pounding in his ears. He sure hoped

nobody would say anything about his little lecture.

Sure enough, somebody did. "Tiki was just telling us not to get ahead of ourselves," Manny piped up.

"Yeah, and how we've got to take it one game at a time," Justin added.

"Really good advice, dude," Luke put in.

"He said all that, huh?" Ronde turned to Tiki with a hurt look in his eyes. "You come up with that all by yourself, big man?" he asked pointedly.

Tiki was silent, embarrassed. He almost wished Ronde would tell them the truth, but Ronde said nothing. He just started eating, never taking his eyes off Tiki.

After a few minutes Tiki couldn't take the silent treatment anymore. "I'm going to study hall," he told them all, getting up with his tray in one hand and his book bag slung over one shoulder. "I've got to go write my essay."

"You're not done with that?" Manny asked.

"I haven't even started." Tiki left, not daring to look at his brother.

Why had he acted so stupidly? He felt like kicking himself. It was bad enough he was bigger than his twin. Did he have to go stealing credit for things too? Tiki made his mind up that the next time he saw any of them, he would give Ronde full credit, first thing.

He sat at his desk in study hall and sighed. Not only did he feel awful, but the gray goo he'd eaten for lunch was now rolling over and over in his stomach.

Tiki stared at the blank page. "Play proud," he said to himself. "Now, what can I say about that?"

He thought for a long moment, and then began to write:

*My mother always tells me and my twin, Ronde, to play proud. She's talking about our football games, but her words mean so much more than that. . . .*

He went on writing until the bell rang. He was concentrating so hard, and writing so fast, that he barely noticed the bell. Mr. Hickey had to shake him by the shoulder to remind him that if he didn't move, he'd be late for fifth period.

Tiki wasn't finished, but close enough. He could put the finishing touches on it that night before bed. More important, he liked what he'd written. Even if he got an F on it, he didn't care. He'd given it his very best, and if that wasn't good enough, so be it.

After all, wasn't that the real meaning of the saying "Play proud"?

The next morning Tiki handed in his finished essay along with everyone else. "Thank goodness that's over with," he muttered as he went back to his desk.

Little did he know how wrong he was. . . .

On Thursday, the day before the Eagles' big game against the mighty Rockets of North Side Junior High, Tiki was heading to the locker room for practice when he heard Dr. Anand calling him.

"Tiki! Tiki Barber!" she said, waving to him from the door of her office. "Will you come here for a moment, please?"

"Me?"

She smiled. "Do you know any other Tiki Barbers around here?"

"At least she isn't mad at me," Tiki said to himself. Going to the principal's office wasn't something a kid normally looked forward to.

"Come in and sit down," she told him, shutting the door behind them and taking a seat behind her desk.

Tiki sat, and then, to his horror, he saw his essay sitting right there on her desk.

Oh, no! Was it something he'd written? Had he used a bad word, or somehow written something stupid?

"Tiki," Dr. Anand began, "your essay was fascinating to read. I must say I didn't expect this from you."

He felt the blood rushing to his face, and he could hear his heart pounding in his ears. Was she about to punish him?

"We received a lot of very good essays this week. In fact, your brother Ronde's was one of three that won honorable mention, but *yours*, Tiki—yours was the best in the whole school. You've won first prize. Congratulations!"

"Say *what*?" Tiki's jaw dropped. He must have looked silly, because she broke out into a pleased laugh.

"I'm amazed you've never shown us this talent of

yours before, young man," she said. "We all knew you were terrific at sports, and a good student, but this—this is truly magnificent."

"Th-thank you," Tiki managed to whisper, still in shock.

"We will now submit your winning essay as the school's entry into the national contest. If you win *that*— well, it means a trip to Washington, DC, and an audience with the president himself! But of course, there are *thousands* of schools competing."

"Oh," said Tiki, "that's okay." If he ever *really* got to meet the president of the United States, he was pretty sure he'd be totally speechless!

"However, I think your essay is so special that it would be a crime to take no note of your achievement."

"My . . . achievement?"

"Yes. So I've decided to call a special assembly for the whole school to honor you."

"Me?" said Tiki, his voice cracking. He was beginning to feel distinctly queasy.

"Yes! And to cap it all, I want you to get up onstage and read your essay out loud."

"*What?* You mean, like, in front of *everybody*?"

Tiki leapt up from his chair and was about to protest, but Dr. Anand didn't give him the chance.

"People who write well should be *proud* to share their ideas," she said. "You've made us all proud, Tiki, and tomorrow you're going to make us even prouder."

He rose slowly, and started out of the room, feeling like someone had hit him in the head with a brick.

"Oh, and, Tiki?"

He turned to face her, but said nothing.

"Good luck in the game tomorrow."

He stared at her as if she was from Mars. "Game? Oh. Yeah. Game. . . . Thanks."

He walked out of her office and into a world of dread. One thought, and one only, filled his brain:

*How am I ever going to get out of this?*

# CHAPTER FIVE

## NO ESCAPE

---

*"OH, NO. NO WAY. NOOOO WAY!"*

"Please. Pretty, pretty pleeeeze, Ronde?"

"Tiki, I am not going to stand up onstage and read your speech for you! Why would I do that? Do I look insane to you?"

"Ronde, you're my *brother*! We do lots of stuff for each other."

"Not *this* kind of stuff."

The two boys were in their darkened bedroom. It was just past lights-out, but neither of them was going to get any sleep until this argument was over.

"I'll do anything you want," Tiki promised. "I'll be your servant for a week!"

"Nuh-uh."

"A month!"

"Stop it, dude," Ronde said firmly. "You're embarrassing yourself. Remember, you got yourself into this mess by writing a better essay than me."

"What are you talking about?" Tiki objected. "I read your essay. It was fine."

"Oh, yeah?"

"It was really good, in fact."

"What did you like best about it?" Ronde goaded him on.

"Oh, that part where you talk about how being smaller means you can surprise the receivers when you jump higher than they do."

Ronde was pleased. That was his favorite part of his essay too. "What else?"

"Oh, yeah. When you said how we're *all* really small, next to the size of the universe."

"Yeah," said Ronde. "I like that part too. But I'm still not giving your speech for you."

"*What?* Why?" Tiki moaned.

"You know what the best, best, best part of being small is?" Ronde asked. Then he answered his own question. "It means I can't pretend to be *you* anymore, so there's no way I could ever get away with reading your essay for you!"

"AAARGH!" With a roar Tiki leapt out of his bed, grabbed his pillow, and started to pummel Ronde with it.

Laughing, Ronde half-tried to protect himself, but he understood how his twin felt. He was just glad it wasn't him who'd won the contest. Honorable mention was plenty good enough, he thought, letting Tiki tire himself out.

"Man," Tiki finally groaned, "why did I have to win that contest?"

"Hey, your essay was the best in the whole school. I don't think anybody's going to think it's stupid."

"Did *you*?" Tiki asked, going back over to his own bed and getting under the covers.

"No! It was right on! People are gonna love it."

"Yeah, sure," Tiki said, then added, "I'm doomed. *Doomed*."

"Hey, look on the bright side," Ronde offered. "When we grow up, if you don't make the NFL, you could always be a writer, or a public speaker. Maybe even a famous actor or something."

"I *am* making the NFL," Tiki shot back. "And so are you. We've got to keep faith in our dream, yo."

"True," Ronde agreed. "But I'm just saying. It's good to have a plan B."

"Nuh-uh," Tiki said. "Not for me. It's plan A all the way. That's the only way to make your dreams come true."

Ronde was silent. In a way he agreed with Tiki. But he also knew that sometimes people's dreams didn't come true. There were millions of kids all over the USA whose dream was to play in the NFL. But only a couple hundred a year would ever get drafted. For all those others, plan B was going to be really important.

"Don't be afraid," Ronde said quietly into the silence of the darkened room. "You'll be fine. You can do it, dude. When you're up there, just think 'Play proud!'"

There was a long silence, then, almost in a whisper, "Thanks, Ronde."

In the morning Ronde woke up, bright and chipper. He washed, got dressed, and was almost on his way down to breakfast when he noticed that Tiki was still under the covers, lying there with his eyes closed and a pained look on his face.

"Hey, what's up?" Ronde asked.

"Ooohhhh," Tiki moaned. "I'm *sooo siiick*."

Ronde blinked, and cocked his head to one side. "What's wrong with you?"

"My head feels like there's an axe stuck in it! And my stomach . . . ooohhh, my stomach . . ."

"MOM!" Ronde yelled. Seconds later her footsteps sounded on the stairs.

"What's going on?" she called to them.

"Tiki's pretending to be sick."

"I'm NOT pretending!" Tiki shouted. "Ma, I'm really sick! Really!"

She came into the room, looked him over, frowned, and felt his forehead. "Hmm. You don't have a fever."

"But my head is pounding!"

"Your tongue's not coated."

"But I'm nauseous!"

"He just doesn't want to read his essay in front of the whole school," Ronde told her.

"Shut up!" Tiki yelled, trying to sock Ronde in the arm.

Ronde dodged the blow, and added, "Everyone's expecting him to be there, Mom. The whole assembly is just to honor *him*!"

"I know all about it," she said. "I tried to get off work today, because I wanted so much to be there." She turned to Tiki, who looked like he was about to cry.

"Why does nobody believe me?" he complained.

"Tiki Barber, look me in the eye. Are you sick, or are you just scared to death?"

He frowned, sitting up in bed. "I'm *not* scared!"

"That's what I thought," she said, smiling. "My boys are brave. They wouldn't let something like giving a speech scare them. Why, you didn't even have to memorize it. You can just read what you already wrote!"

"But, Mom—"

"Tiki, you get dressed now and go to school. If you're still sick after the assembly, you go straight to the nurse's office, all right?"

Tiki sighed deeply and stared at the wall.

"Good," said Mrs. Barber. "Now let's get moving, or we'll all be late."

"I'm going to get you back for this," Tiki told Ronde after she'd left the room.

"Come on," said Ronde. "You know you were faking it."

"Why'd you have to tell her that?"

"You think she wouldn't have known? Dude, she knows *everything*. Have either of us ever faked her out?"

Tiki frowned. Ronde was right, and he knew it.

"Come on." Ronde offered a hand to help him out of bed. "Look at it this way. Those kids *need* to hear your essay."

"Yeah? Well, why do they have to hear it from *me*? Why don't they just publish it in the school paper—under a fake name?"

"You know what?" said Ronde. "They probably will publish it. But you know your name's gonna be on it."

# CHAPTER SIX

## FAME

---

"*. . . AND SO, TO SUM IT ALL UP, WHAT DOES THE* saying 'Play proud' mean? It means playing—and working, and learning, and doing, and helping, and everything else—in a proud way. And what does 'proud' mean?"

Tiki looked up from his paper, which sat on the lectern in front of him. They were all out there—every kid he knew, every teacher, even the photographer from the *Roanoke Reporter*—and there was not a sound in the whole auditorium.

When he'd first stepped up to the lectern, he'd been so nervous he didn't know if his legs would give out underneath him. He had no idea whether his voice would even come out, let alone if it would crack like it sometimes did lately.

The worst thing would have been if they'd laughed at him. He didn't think they'd throw stuff. Everyone pretty much liked him, after all, especially now that he was the school's number one football hero.

But this deathly silence was worse than laughing! He didn't know if it was because they loved the speech or hated it. They weren't smiling—but then, it wasn't a funny speech.

His voice hadn't disappeared on him, and it had cracked only twice—which had drawn a giggle or two— but it had been shaking since he'd first begun his speech. The quiver in his voice was obvious, at least to him, but no one in the crowd seemed to notice.

His essay was only five pages long, but it felt like he'd been speaking for hours and hours. Now, near the end, he felt like racing through the rest of it. But he didn't. Scared as he was, he wanted to make sure they understood what he was trying to say.

Ordering himself to calm down, he cleared his throat and continued.

"What does 'proud' mean? It doesn't mean thinking you're all that, or that you're better than anybody else. The kind of proud my mom means is the kind you have when you're *alone*. When you lie in bed at night, are you proud of how you acted that day? Are you proud of what you said? Would you do it the same way again if you got to do it over?

"For me, playing proud means doing my best. Not just on the field. And not just when I feel like it either. I try to play proud all the time. I know I don't always succeed, but . . . well, I try. And I know that you can learn more from the losses than the wins. And I don't stop trying just because I'm tired. Because even though I might not feel like it, somebody else out there might need me to do my best.

"I know 'Play proud' isn't really such a famous saying, but I think it *should* be. I'm proud of my mom for inventing it. I'm proud of her for living it, every single day. I'm proud . . . to be her son. . . ."

He had to stop for a second, to keep himself from getting too emotional. Taking a deep breath, he finished, "And I hope I'll always play proud enough to make her proud of me."

He stopped, blinked twice, and then looked up at the crowd. For a long, horrible moment nothing happened. *Did they hate it that bad?* he wondered.

And then someone started clapping. Then more people joined in. A few people leapt to their feet, cheering. More rose from their seats, and still more, until every single person in the auditorium had risen to give Tiki a standing ovation! A thunderous roar broke from everyone's lips as they cheered Tiki and his prize-winning essay.

Tiki could not believe it. He was numb from head to toe. Dr. Anand had to guide him back to his chair on the stage. He collapsed into it, while she went to the microphone and asked for another round of applause for Tiki. He nodded weakly in response.

Dr. Anand ended the assembly, and the rows of kids began filing out of the auditorium. The hall instantly grew so loud with chatter that it was impossible to hear anything distinctly.

Tiki nodded and smiled as Dr. Anand, the dean, the assistant principal, the head of the English department, and Ms. Adair all shook his hand and said nice things he couldn't hear over the racket.

Finally he managed to worm his way off the stage and out into the hallway. He was already late. The team bus was waiting. If he didn't hurry to the locker room and grab his stuff, all the players would be sitting in that hot bus, wondering what was keeping him. Tiki didn't want to hold up the whole works right before the big game.

But getting to the locker room wasn't so easy. Not on this day. Kids were everywhere in the hallways, and it seemed like they *all* wanted to talk to Tiki.

"Dude, that was awesome!" Matt Dwayne said, giving him a fist bump and grinning widely. "Who knew you had it in you?"

Tiki looked down at his feet and shrugged.

"Hey, don't be modest," Matt told him. "Be proud, like you said in the speech!"

Tiki looked up at him and nodded. "You're right, man," he said. "It's just . . . I don't know . . ."

"Not used to all the attention?" asked Charlene Shiobara, the head cheerleader. "You should be, after last season. Mr. MVP," she added with a wink.

"*Half* an MVP," Tiki countered, reminding her that he had split the award with Ronde.

"Dude," Matt said, "I've gotta ask you—because this

kid I know has really been getting me angry, and, well, maybe you could help me figure out how to handle it."

"Me?"

"Hey, you obviously know a lot about stuff besides football. I'd just like to get your advice."

"Sure, but I'm late for—"

Charlene's sister Suzie, a seventh grader, was standing next to them, taking it all in. "Could *I* ask you a question?" she asked shyly.

"Sure, but not now. I've got to get to—"

But Suzie wasn't listening. She'd already launched into her question. "I've got this teacher? And she said something mean to me in front of the whole class. How am I supposed to act proud after that?"

Tiki, who was just about to give her the brush-off so he could get to the bus, stopped. "Whoa. Let me think about that, okay?"

"Okay. I could really use some advice," Suzie said. "It's been bugging me, but I didn't know who to ask for help. But you're so . . . so . . ."

"So smart!" Charlene finished for her.

"Yeah, he's the official wise man of Hidden Valley Junior High!" Matt joked.

"Very funny," Tiki said, not laughing. "I've gotta go, you all. See you around."

"Don't forget my question!" Suzie called after him.

"Mine, too!" Matt yelled.

But Tiki was already running down the hallway. He had to keep dodging kids who were coming the other way. He pretended they were defenders on the football field, and showed them his mind-boggling moves, drawing hoots and cheers as he went.

But Suzie's and Matt's words stuck in his mind, even as he gathered his things and took his seat on the bus. He kept wondering if he'd gotten himself into something deeper than he'd ever imagined.

Glancing over at Ronde, who was clowning around with a bunch of the guys in back, Tiki thought, He's *the one who's always got everything figured out.*

As he sat there, Tiki broke into a grin. Yes! *That* was how he'd handle all these questions from kids he barely knew. He'd ask *Ronde* what *he* thought!

Having come to this decision, Tiki relaxed for the first time since Dr. Anand had told him he'd have to give the speech. Yes. Ronde would help him out of this pickle. For now he could let go of his worries, and concentrate on what really mattered—

Football!


The North Side Rockets were a familiar opponent. This was both a good thing and a bad one, thought Tiki.

On the good side, some of the Eagles' greatest, most heroic victories had come against these same Rockets. The Eagles had beaten them in the last game of the season to make the play-offs—a slushfest in the middle of an early snowstorm, in which lucky bounces had meant everything. Only a long last-second field goal from their incredible kicker, Adam Costa, had saved the game for the Eagles that day.

Then the two teams had met up again in the first game of the playoffs. This time there had been no snow or slush, but the game had been just as close. The Eagles had had to come from behind again, and score another last-minute win, the first giant step on the way to their state championship.

Okay, so that was the good side. The bad part was that, having beaten them twice, the Eagles were superconfident they had the Rockets' number.

"We're gonna go off on them so bad!" Paco was saying as the bus bounced and jostled its way down the avenue toward North Side, which was clear on the other end of Roanoke. "I can't wait for this game to start!"

"They've got no game," Justin Landzberg said, nodding in agreement. "I say we come out ahead by three TDs."

"Four, baby," said Manny.

"Four plus three for a field goal," Adam chimed in.

"Oh, yeah!" Paco said, clapping and laughing. "We've *got* this. Have we got this? *Yes,* we've got this!"

Tiki frowned. He was glad they were confident, but all that trash talk worried him—a *lot.* He'd warned them about it, but he guessed they hadn't really been listening. Or else they just couldn't help themselves. Either way, it made him feel anxious.

Coach Wheeler wasn't really paying attention. He had his nose in the playbook, putting the finishing touches on his game plan. Tiki glanced over at Ronde, and could tell from the look on his face that his twin was feeling the same way.

There was a difference between confidence and *over-confidence*. And the Eagles were close to crossing that line, if they hadn't already.

Sure enough, the game had barely started when they made a huge mistake. On the first play from scrimmage, following a short kickoff return from Ronde, Manny Alvaro fumbled the snap from Paco!

The ball was kicked by someone, and wound up bouncing straight to one of the defenders, who fell on it and covered it like it was a sack of gold.

Tiki let out a loud groan. He noticed the shock in the eyes of his teammates as they trotted off to the sideline. A bad start, but it was still early. They could easily turn things back around, *if* their heads were in the right place.

Coach Wheeler barked, "Come on, Eagles. Concentrate! We've drilled this all week! Fundamentals! Fundamentals!"

Tiki frowned. Coach didn't usually get this frustrated. He could see that Wheeler, too, felt the pressure of being defending champs.

When you were on top, everyone else was going to bring their "A" game when they played against you. You weren't going to get any sympathy if you messed up, either.

Last season they'd been underdogs, but they'd stuck together, kept their eyes on the prize, and yes, they'd gotten lucky more than once. But this year was different. And it was quickly becoming obvious just *how* different.

The Rockets offense was made up mostly of returning ninth graders. They were experienced and talented, and had played together for two years now.

The Eagles had a lot of new faces, young players without much game experience. The rookies might have been talented—even more talented than the kids they'd replaced—but they hadn't played together for very long, and football is, above all, a *team* game.

And so the Rockets were able to take advantage of the Eagles' inexperience. With trick play after trick play, the Rockets scored a series of big gains that took them to the Eagle thirteen yard line. Then they flooded Ronde's zone with receivers, creating a crowd that got between Ronde and his man, blocking him off from the play and allowing the Rockets to complete an easy touchdown pass!

The home crowd went wild, cheering their Rockets, while the gloomy Eagles defense walked slowly back to the bench after the extra point. The team was now trailing 7–0, and they looked like a bunch of beginners!

Coach Wheeler was not happy. "Ronde, you're the captain out there," he said. "Sound off if guys are getting in your way, or if you need to switch off to keep them covered."

Ronde nodded but didn't answer.

"Okay, kid. Let's get those points back!" Coach Wheeler clapped Ronde on the back and sent him out to receive the kickoff.

This time the blockers in front of Ronde whiffed on their blocks, letting the Rockets run right by them. The Rockets piled onto Ronde before he could take a single step! He held on to the ball, thank goodness.

Tiki trotted back onto the field. He was determined to say something to his teammates. Just as Ronde was defensive captain, Tiki was the on-field general of the offense this season.

"Okay, guys," he said as they huddled up. "Let's just play it like we do in practice. Everybody stick your blocks and hold your lanes. Manny and I will do the rest."

They all clapped once, and Manny read out the play. An off-tackle run for Tiki, with Justin as lead blocker. The play gained four yards—nothing spectacular, but at least they hadn't coughed up the ball or been thrown for a loss. It was a small confidence-builder, but at least it was something.

Next Manny fired a bullet to Felix for a first down, and the Eagles were off and running. They pounded the ball on the ground, play after play, with Tiki and Justin taking turns carrying the ball.

The clock kept running. By the time it had ticked down to five minutes, the Eagles were knocking at the door, first and goal at the eight yard line.

Now it was time for one of their favorite plays, a fake handoff followed by Manny rolling out on the QB option. He could either fire it to Tiki or turn the corner and hug the sideline all the way to the end zone.

This time Manny chose to keep it himself. It was a split-second decision, and it was the wrong one. A Rockets defender hit him low, upending Manny, who went head over heels, with the ball flying loose.

Again, a Rockets defender pounced on it—one of their safeties this time. Instead of simply falling on the ball, he grabbed it in full stride and ran all the way back upfield for another Rockets touchdown!

Tiki fell to his knees and grabbed his helmet with both hands, letting out a strangled cry of frustration. "Nooooo! I was wide open!" he shouted to no one in particular.

Shaking his head, he followed his teammates back to the bench. Ronde passed him on his way to receive yet another kickoff, shaking his head slowly and silently.

This was not the start that any of them had envisioned. This was a flat-out disaster!

Looking up and down the bench, Tiki saw his teammates all staring at the ground between their legs. It was hot, and everyone looked like a tired old dog, ready to slink away and hide in the shade.

"Get up!" Tiki suddenly found himself yelling. Waving his arms, one of which held his helmet, he repeated, "Get up! Everybody, get up and fire up Ronde with some noise!"

Slowly, one by one, the Eagles rose to their feet. "Let's go, Ronde!" one of them shouted. "Come on, Ronde!"

"Woo-hoo!"

By the time the kick went up, there was at least as much noise coming from the Eagles as from the Rockets fans in the stands. Tiki didn't know whether Ronde could hear them, but he sure hoped he could feel the support coming his way.

Ronde grabbed the ball and made a quick, dazzling fake to his right, then spun around and ran left. He turned the corner, skipped by a defender, and sped down the sideline, with three Rockets trailing after him.

"GO, RONDE!!!" Tiki yelled along with all the other Eagles.

They were jumping up and down now, all right. Ronde had taken their energy and thrown it right back at them, double! By the time he was finally tackled, he had run the ball all the way to the Rockets seventeen!

Tiki sped onto the field, the rest of the offense right behind him. He couldn't wait to get the ball into his hands again. "Notre Dame, on one," said Manny to the huddled Eagles.

*Good.* A quick lateral to Tiki, with the blocking leading him to the right.

Tiki grabbed the ball in midair, but one of the Rockets linebackers, who obviously remembered the play from last season, was right there to stuff it!

Still behind the line of scrimmage, Tiki made a split-second decision and faked a halfback pass. The linebacker leapt into the air to block it, and Tiki had him right where he wanted him. Before the kid came down to earth, Tiki had blown right past him and made it all the way to the five yard line!

On the very next play Manny faked it to him, then rolled left, hiding the ball while the defenders piled onto Tiki. By the time he got up, the score was 14–6, with Adam's extra point to follow. The Eagles were right back in it!

Unfortunately, the Rockets had been on offense most of the game, and the Eagle defenders were tired. It showed in the next series, with the Rockets driving the length of the field, and scoring another easy touchdown against the young, inexperienced Eagles defense.

Ronde looked like he was about to explode. "Keep a lid on it," Tiki advised him. "Take it all out on the Rockets, man."

Ronde nodded, his eyes still full of fire. After running onto the field, he took the kickoff and plowed right through five or six defenders, to put the Eagles back in good field position at their own forty-six.

Tiki led the next drive with a pair of cutback runs—faking one way and then running the other once the defenders had taken the bait. Finally, with the Eagles at the goal line, he took a flying jump over the middle, scoring a touchdown with a leap he would have been too small to make the year before.

That gave Tiki at least *some* satisfaction, but the Eagles were still down a touchdown. Before long the Rockets scored again, after throwing a long bomb over the head of Alister Edwards, the Eagles' free safety.

There was still one minute left in the half. From their own twenty-six, with no time-outs, the Eagles offense took to the air. In this two-minute drill Tiki's job was to protect Manny from any blitzes, and to be available for dump-off passes if Manny couldn't find open receivers.

That's exactly what happened on first down. Tiki had to reach back to get it, and almost got thrown for a loss. Luckily, he managed to shake off that first tackle, which gave him a chance to do some real broken-field running.

Giving up nothing to Ronde, who did this sort of thing every time he ran back a kick, Tiki threw some of his best moves at the defense. That fooled some of them, but one or two Rockets got their hands on him.

And that's when Tiki discovered something important. He wasn't only bigger than he'd been last season, he was also *stronger*. This year he was able to drag the tacklers with him and keep on going.

Finally they gang-tackled him at the five yard line. Tiki sprang right back up and yelled, "Line up! Line up! Spike it, Manny!" Having been on the team for two years, Tiki knew there couldn't be much time left, and the Eagles were already out of time-outs.

Manny spiked the ball, with just two seconds left. Tiki's quick reaction had bought them one more play. Tiki looked over at Coach Wheeler. Would he send in a play, or bring Adam out for an easy field goal?

Tiki was glad when Coach kept Adam on the sideline. With the Eagles down by fourteen, Wheeler wanted every last point he could get. He sent Justin in with the play.

Tiki felt a thrill go through him. Screen pass. To him. *Yes!*

Manny delivered the ball right on target, and Tiki took it from there. Once again he wound up dragging two Rockets with him. This time all the way into the end zone!

The extra point brought the Eagles within a touchdown at the half. But as he trotted off the field with his teammates, Tiki was not in a good mood. Not at all.

No matter how many points they managed to score, if the defense kept giving them up, the Eagles' dream of an undefeated season would be gone before it even got started.

# CHAPTER SEVEN

## THE CAPTAIN SPEAKS

*RONDE FLUNG OPEN THE LOCKER ROOM DOOR*
so hard that it banged. The noise suddenly silenced a
locker room full of worried murmurs.

Taking one look at his teammates' faces, Ronde burst
out, "What in the world was *that*?" as he flung his hands
wide. "Was that football? I don't think so!"

Kids were looking at one another guiltily. "It's not
just one or two of us. It's all of us!" Ronde went on. He
couldn't contain his feelings.

Ronde half-expected Coach Wheeler or one of the
other coaches to grab him, to stop him. But the whole
locker room stayed still and silent. Ronde, the captain of
the Eagle defense, had the floor.

"We may be talented," he said, "but if we keep playing
stupid, we're gonna get beat!" He might have been one of
the smaller players on the field, but no one had a bigger
heart.

"Defense!" he shouted. "When you hit somebody,
you've got to put them on the ground! Receivers, you got
a route to run? Three steps and cut? Then count one, two,

three! If you add a step or cut too quick, the ball's not gonna be there for you.

"You new kids," he said, scanning the room and taking in all the rookies with a fiery glance, "I know you haven't seen much action before. Most times, seventh graders ride the bench their first year, but this year we *need* you guys. And we need you to play like you've been here awhile. Remember what you learned in practice. And okay, you're gonna make mistakes. So *learn* from them, and learn fast, because we've got a mission, and it doesn't include losing."

Finally he looked around the room again, singling out the veterans on the team—his fellow ninth graders. "You guys," he said, "I'm not kidding. We're gonna go nowhere if we don't set an example for these kids. We know how to win, so let's go out there and show it!"

"Yeah!" yelled a few of the Eagles, clapping their hands. Others nodded, while a few were still looking down at their feet.

Coach Wheeler didn't look kindly on players criticizing their teammates. Last year's quarterback, Cody Hansen, had caused several near fights among his teammates that way. Somehow, though, when Ronde spoke up, everyone got quiet and listened.

Ronde looked over at Coach Wheeler, expecting him to be mad. But to his surprise, Coach had a crooked, surprised smile on his face.

"Thank you, Ronde," he said. "Kids, that's your captain speaking, and I couldn't agree more." He turned to Tiki. "You want to add something, Captain?" he asked.

Tiki shook his head. "No, thanks, Coach. I've been giving more than enough speeches lately. And Ronde said it all."

This got an appreciative laugh. They'd all been in the auditorium for Tiki's speech that same afternoon.

"Okay, then," Coach Wheeler said, clapping his hands three times. "We're only down seven points after all that dreadful football we played. So let's get out there and play our game—our *real* game! As Tiki said this afternoon—even if he doesn't want to repeat himself—we've got to play proud!"

"Yeah! Play proud!" several of the Eagles roared.

"Okay, team, get out there!" Wheeler said.

Ronde opened his mouth wide and made as much sound as he could. Then he joined the crush of his teammates, crowding back through the doorway on their way out to the field.

North Side Junior High was a big school—much bigger than Hidden Valley—and they'd always been a football powerhouse. Last year they'd made the play-offs, only to be knocked off by the Eagles in the first round. This year they were out for revenge. They had the Eagles right where they wanted them too—a touchdown behind, away from home. Now they meant to move in for the kill.

Ronde knew it, but he also knew that they wouldn't be expecting a burst of energy from the Eagles coming out of the locker room.

He was right. On the kickoff Ronde flew headlong at the ballcarrier, hitting him square in the upper arm and knocking the ball free.

Ronde didn't see what happened after that (he was quickly smothered by a pair of Rockets), but he could tell by the groan from the crowd that the Eagles had recovered the fumble.

Instead of starting the second half on defense, desperately trying to stop the Rockets from going up by fourteen, the Eagles now had a chance to tie the game. Starting on the Rockets forty yard line, the offense got to work.

Ronde watched from the sidelines, cheering his lungs out as Tiki ran for twelve yards and a first down. It was amazing to see his twin bowl over the opposing players like that. Last year Tiki would have bounced right off them. Now he was much bigger and stronger, and it was the defenders who were getting knocked down!

Ronde felt a brief pang of jealousy. Still skinny and short, he had to make up for it with his speed and leaping ability, knocking the ball away from wide receivers who were six inches taller and fifty pounds heavier.

But for now all Ronde cared about was that Tiki keep on plowing through the defense. "Go, TIKI!" he yelled, making himself hoarse as his twin rushed for another eight tough yards, down to the Rockets twenty.

Next Manny faked a handoff, then rolled to his right and found Frank Amadou in the back of the end zone. Frank made a tremendous leap and came down with the ball, but he landed with one foot out of the end zone! Cheers turned to groans on the Eagles sideline.

But they need not have worried. On the very next play Tiki burst through the line like an bullet, running straight up the gut for an easy touchdown.

"Unstoppable!" Ronde screamed, punching the air. "Yesss!!!"

Adam's kick tied the game, and Ronde strapped his helmet back on. Now it was his turn.

The Rockets went to work from their own twenty yard line. Ronde lined up against their number one wide receiver, Zach Martin. Last season, Martin had scored ten touchdowns in the Rockets' twelve games, as Ronde knew because he studied all the stats. Ronde was good at math, and he knew Zach was seven inches taller than he was.

No matter. Today Zach would not be scoring a single touchdown. He would not be catching any long passes. Not with Ronde covering him like a barnacle on a rock.

On this drive the Rockets kept the ball on the ground, grinding out first downs and eating up the clock. Ronde understood their strategy. It was the same one the Eagles used when they played against high-powered offenses: Keep the ball out of the other team's hands.

It turned out to be a good strategy. The Rockets, taking advantage of the younger Eagles defenders, used fake handoffs, misdirection plays, and draw plays to move the ball into Eagles territory.

At the Eagles twenty-five, with third down and two to go, Ronde got a sudden shiver up his spine. They were going to put it into the air, he just knew it. He could feel it.

Sure enough, the quarterback faked a handoff and then dropped back to pass. Ronde gave his man a vicious bump, sending him sprawling out of bounds. That meant Zach Martin was now out of the play.

Then, seeing that the quarterback was having trouble finding an open man, Ronde went straight for him. He blindsided him just as he was about to throw. The ball flew straight up, and Ronde leapt to grab it. He hauled it in just as a huge offensive lineman slammed him to the turf, but he held on to the ball!

Tiki found him and helped him up. "That's what I call playing proud!" he told Ronde.

"You run that ball in, Brother," Ronde said, gripping his twin's hand in a mutual fist-lock.

"Watch me."

As the ref blew the whistle for play to resume, Ronde ran off the field. He accepted hugs and high fives all around, but he noticed that the players were already watching the offense go to work. This was a determined team, so different from the one that had showed up to play the first half.

Ronde smiled, feeling deeply happy. *This* was the team he remembered from last year—refusing to go down, refusing to lose.

On instructions from Coach Wheeler the offense now went to the air. Manny fired off successive darts to Felix and Luke for a pair of first downs. And then it was Tiki time. After faking a pass to Felix, Manny then dumped the ball off to Tiki along the sideline.

The cornerback went for him, but Tiki just threw him off. The corner crashed into his teammates on the sideline, nearly bowling them over.

Tiki was already down the field, butting headfirst into one of the safeties, knocking him flat on his backside!

This was a totally new Tiki. He still had the cutback moves. But he now also brought another element to his game—brute force.

Ronde could only imagine what Tiki must be feeling now, as he knocked defenders over with sheer strength and determination. But of course, identical twins have an uncanny ability to get inside each other's thoughts, and Tiki and Ronde were no exception.

Ronde watched, holding his breath as Tiki pulled one last spin move and stumbled forward into the end zone. "Woo-hoo!!" Ronde shouted. "Tiiii-kiiii!"

The bleachers were quiet, but the Eagles' sideline erupted in enough noise for a whole stadium. The quarter ended after Adam's extra point, with the Eagles leading for the first time, and the teams switched ends of the field for the kickoff.

Ronde was ready for anything—but not for what happened next. Just as he was about to lay a big hit on the return man, a freight train ran into him from the right and sent him flying. He hit the ground with extreme force, and a body landed on top of him.

"Ooof! Ow, that hurt!" Ronde yelled, pushing the guy off him. As he did so, he was shocked to find that it was one of his own teammates, a new kid on special teams.

"What in the—"

"Sorry. Sorry, Ronde!" the poor kid said, backing off.

Ronde looked down the field, but he already knew what had happened. He could tell by the roar from the stands that the returner had gone all the way for the touchdown.

"I *had* him, man!" Ronde shouted at the kid, who'd obviously made the team because of his speed and strength. He'd sure hit Ronde hard! "What did you think you were doing?"

"I . . . I guess I was running with my head down," said the kid, peeking at Ronde guiltily. "I thought . . . I thought you were . . ."

"You thought I was *him*," Ronde finished for him.

"I said I was sorry," the kid said, on the verge of tears.

"Hey, don't worry about it," Ronde told him, clapping him on the back. "It's gonna be okay. Let's go. We've got a game to finish."

He trotted off to the sideline with the kid right behind him. Just as they got there, North Side kicked the extra point to tie the game back up.

"What's your name again?" Ronde asked him.

"Rio. Rio Ikeda."

"Don't worry, Rio," Ronde told him as they ran back onto the field to receive the kickoff. "I'm gonna get those points back right now, and you're gonna help me."

"Me?"

"Just stay to my right the whole time," Ronde told him. "And look alive."

"Huh?"

"Stay alert. You never know what I might do."

The kid looked puzzled, but he did as he was told and lined up to the right of Ronde.

Grabbing the kick, Ronde took off to his left. There was no time to check if Rio was to his right. The Rockets were after him, and closing fast!

Ronde turned the corner and headed downfield. He leapt over one Rocket who was sprawled on the ground beneath him, and made another defender miss, but soon he saw that the jig was up. Two Rockets were about to slam into him.

That's when he wheeled around and tossed the football—right into the arms of a shocked Rio, who was trailing Ronde, just as he was supposed to. Rio was so surprised that he almost dropped the ball.

But he didn't. Remembering Ronde's warning, he stayed alert, and when the ball suddenly came his way, he was able to react in time.

The defenders slammed into Ronde, but he was no longer the man with the ball. All by himself Rio now put his exceptional speed to work. By the time the Rockets could react, he was three steps past them, racing untouched the rest of the way to the end zone!

Again Ronde knew from the moan of the crowd that his trick had worked. Not only had he put his team back out front, but he'd turned a lemon into lemonade, helping Rio Ikeda go from zero to hero in one single play!

Adam kicked the extra point, and the Eagles now spent the rest of the fourth quarter fending off a ferocious Rockets counterattack.

The game ended with a Hail Mary pass that wound up getting intercepted by Alister Edwards, another new starter making another big play!

In the end the Eagles had their victory. It had been hard won, but to Ronde it was very satisfying. He and Tiki had brought their "A" game, and Ronde's speech at halftime had made all the difference in the world.

Play proud. It was funny, thought Ronde, how his speech had had the same message as Tiki's.

But really, the saying didn't belong to either one of them.

It was their mom's.

# CHAPTER EIGHT

## THE WEIGHT OF THE WORLD

---

**AS TIKI RODE THE BUS TO SCHOOL MONDAY** morning, his mind was troubled. All the other kids were horsing around, laughing, making lots of noise—but Tiki just stared out the window, watching the streets of Roanoke roll by.

He knew he should be happy, but he wasn't. Sure, he had a lot to be happy about at Hidden Valley—a football starter, the winner of the essay contest, taller and bigger and stronger than his identical twin—but the Eagles and their future crowded his thoughts.

Yes, they'd won their first two games. But this last one had been a real nail-biter. The Eagles could easily have lost. They'd been behind at halftime, and their many rookies and eighth graders had made a ton of mistakes. Ronde had had to throw a fit to get them to play their best in the second half, and even then the Eagles had barely pulled out the victory.

What was it going to be like next time they fell behind? Because it was a long season, and Tiki knew they would not always have a big lead to sit on. Were locker room explosions going to be a regular feature? And would they always work to inspire the team?

Tiki thought not. Getting yelled at once might get you to play harder, but getting yelled at all the time was no good for anything. You just got down in the dumps and played worse.

The Eagles locker room had been happy after the game. But he wondered if some of the players were mad at Ronde now. He guessed he'd find out at practice if there were lasting hard feelings, but he knew for sure that things had better improve if the Eagles wanted to repeat as champs, let alone have an undefeated season.

That was another thing that bothered him. All this talk about going undefeated was no good. It made them think about the distant future instead of concentrating on this game, this play, this moment.

There was so much he wanted to say to his team-mates. Maybe he'd give another speech, just for them, he thought. Then he shuddered at the vision. Giving speeches was not his thing, even if he had done well at it last week.

He filed off the bus with the rest of the kids, still full of worry. But before he could duck inside the school building, he was waylaid by Laura Sommer. "Hel-lo! Earth to Tiki?" she began, grabbing him by the arm and turning him to face her.

Laura was tall with long blond hair, and had thick

glasses with black frames that sat off-kilter on her nose. "We need to talk," she said in a tone that didn't allow for argument.

She practically dragged him off to the side, until they were standing next to the big elm tree that shaded the school entrance. "What's up?" he asked her.

"I have a favor to ask you," she began.

"Uh . . . okay." She probably wanted to do an interview with him for the school paper, he figured. Something about winning the prize and giving the speech.

"We're always looking for a new angle, for something different," she explained, motioning with both arms like she was showing him the shape of a newspaper. "And we've decided—'we' meaning me, Mrs. Flanagan, and the rest of the editors—that we'd like you to join the staff of the *Weekly Eagle!*"

"What? *Me?* I don't—"

He was about to say that he didn't get it, but she didn't give him time.

"We've been looking to do an advice column. You know, answering letters from kids who have problems. And we thought, who better than you?"

"Huh?"

"You were so great giving that speech—everyone thought so—and you obviously understand so much about everything."

"But I—"

"And I hear kids have already started asking you for advice. So we figured you could be our new star columnist! Say yes, okay? Good. It's a deal."

She grabbed his limp hand and shook it, like it meant they had a deal. Laura was persuasive, Tiki had to give her that. Pushy, some would have said.

"I—"

"Great!" she chirped, giving him a big smile full of braces. "So we'll print an announcement in this week's paper, asking for letters to be sent to 'Dear Tiki,' and then you can start answering them in the next edition!"

She clapped her hands together and squealed with joy, jumping up and down. "Fantastic!"

"I, um . . ."

"Great. I've gotta go," she said, trying to escape with her victory intact.

But Tiki snapped out of it just in time. Grabbing her by the arm before she could get away, he said, "Hold up, Laura. Wait a second."

"I've gotta get to class," she said, looking worried.

"Yeah. Me too. It's just—I don't know about this."

"What?"

"You know, this job. I don't know if I'm cut out for it."

"What do you mean? You're perfect for it! We all agreed!"

"I didn't agree."

"Sure you did. You just did! I'm a witness!"

"No, no, no, no, no," Tiki said, shaking his head. "I never said anything."

"So you didn't say no, either."

"Not yet," he said.

"Great! So I've gotta go."

"Just a second," he repeated, hanging on to her arm.

Just then Suzie Shiobara came up to them. "Hi, Tiki," she said. "Did you think about my question?"

Tiki's jaw dropped. He'd forgotten all about it. He'd kinda promised her an answer, but he hadn't even thought about her problem!

"Uh, yeah, I've been giving it a lot of thought," he said, stalling.

"And?"

"Well, it's complicated, and I've got to get to class."

Suzie's face fell. "This is so important to me," she said. "And I was counting on your advice."

Laura's eyes lit up. "Well, guess what? Tiki's going to be doing the advice column for the *Weekly Eagle*! He can answer your question in this week's edition, since he's already got your question. The paper comes out day after tomorrow! Right, Tiki?"

She turned to Tiki and cocked her head questioningly. Tiki looked from her to Suzie and back again, then swallowed hard. "Uh, I guess," he said, flashing Suzie a big smile.

"Of course, your privacy will be totally respected,"

Laura told Suzie. "No names or anything—strictly anonymous."

*Except for me,* thought Tiki miserably. How had he ever let himself get talked into this? *Man,* he thought, shaking his head as he headed for homeroom. *I wish I'd never won that essay contest.*

"What's wrong with you?"

"Nothing, Ronde," Tiki said grumpily. "Let me be. I'm trying to think."

"What are you doing? Homework?"

"Sort of. Quit looking over my shoulder!"

"What?" Ronde pushed away the arm Tiki was using to hide his notebook. "What are you doing, writing a love letter?"

"Shut up!" Tiki said, giving Ronde a shove.

"If it isn't, then, why are you hiding it?"

"I'm not hiding it," Tiki said. "There. See for yourself." He took his hand away and let Ronde have a good look at his first "Dear Tiki" column.

"What is this?" Ronde said, screwing up his face in confusion. "Who is 'Dear Troubled'?"

"That's the girl who sent in the letter."

"What letter? What do you mean, 'sent in'?"

Tiki sighed. "It's an advice column. For the *Weekly Eagle.* You know, like 'Dear Abby.' Only this one is 'Dear Tiki.'"

"Oh, that is so lame," Ronde said, shaking his head. "Tell me you're not doing that."

"I am," Tiki said, sighing. "I got myself roped into it."

"By who?"

"Laura Sommer."

"Ooohhhh," Ronde said, understanding at once how Tiki could have gotten himself cornered into something like this. Laura was not a person who took no for an answer.

"All right. Have a look, since you're so nosey anyway," Tiki said. "Maybe you can even help me out."

"Oh, no. Don't look at me," Ronde said, backing away. "I don't even want to *see* it. You're not getting me involved. No way."

"Don't you want to help other kids with their problems?"

"Hey, don't look at me," Ronde said. "You're the prize-winning writer."

"You won honorable mention, remember?" Tiki pleaded. "And you're always the one who gives the best advice. Look what happened in the locker room at halftime!"

"I was just telling them what you said in your essay," Ronde shot back.

"Come on, Ronde!" Tiki begged. "I need a little help!"

"A little help?" Ronde said. "Okay, I'll give you a little advice. If you want something done right, do it yourself. Now, *that's* a famous saying!"

"Ronde . . ."

"I've gotta go watch TV. My favorite show's on in five minutes."

Before Tiki could stop him, Ronde was off to the living room, leaving him alone in the kitchen. The remains of their dinner were still on the table. He and Ronde would have to clean up and wash the dishes before their mom got home from work.

She'd left their dinner for them, as she always did when she worked late. Tiki knew he shouldn't complain about his own problems. Their mom had it much harder than either of them—two jobs, and she never complained. Ever.

Sighing, Tiki took up his pen again and tried to think of an answer to Suzie's problem.

*Dear Tiki,* her letter to him began. (He'd written it himself, based on what she'd asked him in person.) *I have a problem. My teacher is always being mean to me. What should I do? Signed, Troubled.*

*Dear Troubled,* Tiki had begun his reply. But that was as far as he'd gotten. He had no idea what Suzie should do about her mean teacher. Sometimes teachers were just mean, or they just didn't happen to like you, and what could you do about that except just take it?

He squeezed his eyes shut, searching for a better response, something that would make Suzie feel better, even if it didn't make her problem go away. Finally something came to him:

Dear Troubled,

I know how you must feel. I mean, we've all had teachers we weren't wild about. They're like the rest of us, really. They sometimes have bad days, and say stuff they're probably sorry for later. But it's not okay for your teacher to call you out in front of the whole class. Hurting your feelings isn't going to help you learn better.

I know it hurts, but telling everyone how mean your teacher is won't solve your problem, and it might make things even worse.

My suggestion is that you hold your head up, even when your teacher makes fun of you, or other kids laugh at you. Also, I advise you to write a private note to your teacher. Tell him or her how you felt when they made fun of you. I'm sure if they knew, they'd feel sorry about it and wouldn't do it again. At least I hope not.

If this doesn't work, and they only get meaner to you, then you've got a real problem and you should probably tell the principal, or at least your parents. Good luck, Troubled, and let me know how it works out!

Tiki put down his pen and shook out his hand, which was starting to cramp. Had he really just written all that? Thinking back, he couldn't recall a time when he'd written that much, straight out of his head, in one quick shot. Had it really taken him only ten minutes?

After closing his notebook, he went to join Ronde in

the living room. There'd be time to do the dishes after they were done watching TV.

Ronde was shocked to see him. "What, did you give up already?" he asked.

"I'm done."

"What?"

"I did it."

"You mean . . . ?"

"Yeah, man. It's finished."

"Can I read it?"

"You can read it—in the *Weekly Eagle*, like everybody else."

"Hey!"

"Hey, my foot. If you wanted to see it in advance, you should have helped me do it."

So saying, he plopped down at Ronde's side. "So," he said, grinning, "what'd I miss?"


The next day Tiki stopped into the newspaper office after school to drop off his column before going down to football practice.

"How'd it go?" Laura asked him, her eyes twinkling behind her glasses.

"Okay, I guess," he told her, handing over the page from his notebook.

"Everyone's really excited about this," Laura said

brightly. "I told some kids in PE, and a bunch of them said they were going to write in and ask for advice. Pretty soon you're gonna have six letters a week!"

Tiki felt sick to his stomach. "Six? No way."

"Yes way!" she replied, giving his arm a squeeze. "You're already a success, and you haven't even had your first column in print. Wowie-zowie!!"

"Yeah," Tiki mumbled. "Wowie . . . whatever."

"Do you want to see how we do the pasteup and lay-out?" she offered.

"Uh, some other time, okay?" he said, his stomach churning. "I've got to get to practice."

"Oh! Right. Of course. I forgot about the football thing. . . . Well, see ya!"

Tiki got out of there as quickly as he could. Six letters a week!? It might as well have been a mountain of them crashing down on his head.

Sure, it had taken him only ten minutes to do that first response, but he couldn't count on ideas coming to him that fast all the time! When he'd agreed to do the column, he'd thought it would be only one letter a week, or two at most.

"The football thing," as Laura had called it, was way more important to him, and it took up most of his free time. How was he supposed to handle all this extra responsibility?

He arrived in the locker room still feeling anxious, although his stomach was no longer threatening to turn over. He dressed in his practice uniform and ran out onto the field, happy to be outside, playing the game he loved, and not thinking about other people's problems.

Except he couldn't seem to shake the thoughts that kept creeping into his brain. He kept seeing Suzie Shiobara, and her sister Charlene, and Matt Dwayne, and the other kids from Laura's PE class, all calling his name, waving pieces of paper that held their problems for him to solve—

*BONK!!*

All of a sudden the football hit him square in the side of the helmet.

"What in the—" Tiki turned to see a half dozen of his teammates laughing their heads off and pointing at him. "What's so funny?"

"Dude," said Manny, who had obviously thrown the pass, "I yelled 'Heads up' three times! Are you in dreamland or what?"

More laughter followed this remark, and that got Tiki annoyed. "I'm not in dreamland, yo. I'm just thinking."

"Well, quit thinking, and concentrate on football for a while instead, huh?" This from Coach Pellugi, head of the Eagles offense, who happened to catch the last part of the conversation. "Let's go, fellas. Look alive. We've got a big game coming up, and we don't want to play like we did the last game."

Coach Ontkos was right, Tiki knew. They'd gotten away with a victory in a game they could have, and maybe *should* have, lost. They might not be so lucky next time.

It was important to practice hard now, to get all the players working together like a well-oiled machine. None of them, least of all Tiki, could afford to spend this precious time daydreaming.

And yet . . . those letters waiting for him on the other side of tomorrow's edition of the *Weekly Eagle* kept swimming into his brain, drawing his concentration away from where it needed to be.

*OOOF!* Manny's handoff caught him by surprise, and he nearly dropped the ball.

"Let's go, Barber!" Coach Pellugi barked. "Everyone works hard today. No exceptions!"

Tiki felt the blood rush to his face. It was a good thing his helmet was on, covering his look of embarrassment.

"Sorry, Coach," he said. "It won't happen again."

He was irritated by his teammates' laughter, even though he knew he had it coming. He'd written to Suzie in his column that she should hold her head up, even when her classmates were laughing at the teacher's cruel remarks. Yet here he was, finding it hard to take his own good advice!

He wondered how that advice would go over. Would people like his new column? Would they think his advice was good? What if they hated it? What if his advice was bad and screwed up someone else's life big-time?

And how was he supposed to concentrate on football with all these worries weighing him down?

# CHAPTER NINE
## WHAT NEXT?

---

*WHEN RONDE SAW TIKI AT LUNCHTIME THAT* Wednesday, it was from a distance. Tiki was surrounded by kids, all of whom were talking to him at once. Most were waving copies of the school paper. One girl wanted his autograph on it. Ronde saw Tiki's startled look as he took her pen and signed his name under his first advice column.

*So,* Ronde thought. Tiki was a star now, and not just at football. He laughed to himself at the strangeness of it all. He was a little jealous, sure. Who wouldn't be? But he was also proud of his brother's success. It was really something, to have everyone admire you, not just for your athletic ability, but for your wisdom, too.

Ronde wondered if maybe he should have taken Tiki up on his offer to help with the column. After all, he was as good as Tiki at giving people advice. He did it all the time, whether they wanted to hear it or not. In fact, when he and Tiki argued, it was Ronde who was right 90 percent of the time.

He gave up on getting anywhere near Tiki for the

moment and settled in at a far-off table with Justin, Paco, and Adam.

"Jeez," Paco was saying, looking over at the crowd that surrounded Tiki. "I sure hope he's got his head in the game when Friday rolls around."

Ronde hadn't thought of it, but Paco had a point. They'd all seen how distracted Tiki'd been at practice, and that was *before* the paper had come out. Now that everyone wanted his advice, would Tiki be able to keep his mind on the game?

Ronde sure hoped so, because their next two opponents were the best teams in the league—Blue Ridge and Pulaski. The Eagles were going to need all of Tiki's energy and effort, not just a part.

After practice Ronde grabbed his brother's arm before they got on the bus. "Let's go for an ice cream soda," he suggested.

"Huh? How are we gonna get home if we do that?"

"It's only a couple miles. We can walk it—or we could race."

"Ha! You know I'd have you beat."

"Yeah?"

"Yeah, but we probably shouldn't run if we're gonna have ice cream sodas first."

"So, is that a yes?" Ronde wondered.

"You buying?"

"Oooo, you got me," Ronde said. Out of his pocket he fished two worn dollar bills he'd earned for mowing Mrs. Prendergast's lawn. "I'm gonna need some help, though. I'm a little short."

"I noticed."

"Hey!"

"Sorry. You set me up for that one."

Tiki searched his own pockets and came up with eighty-five cents. "Mr. Kessler will let us owe him the other fifteen cents," Ronde assured his twin. "Let's go— for old times' sake, huh?"

The twins had been going to Kessler's for sodas and comic books ever since third grade. The place was near their school, but also close to the high school, and to the elementary school they'd both attended. Mr. Kessler had known them since they were little, when they'd been harder to tell apart.

He was always happy to see them, and today was no exception. "Hey, how's my guys?" he asked, coming out from behind the counter and clapping them both on the backs. "You're all over the papers these days. Football heroes! Who would've thought it?"

Looking from one to the other, he frowned in confusion. "Hey, I thought you guys were supposed to be identical."

"I know, I know," Ronde said, sighing in frustration. "He just hit his growth spurt first, is all."

"I'm three inches taller," Tiki said proudly, then put up his hands to meet Ronde's elbow, which otherwise would have poked him in the ribs.

"Well, never mind," Mr. Kessler told Ronde. "You'll catch up soon enough."

"I don't know about the 'soon enough' part," said Ronde, letting it go for now.

"Hey, here come a couple of your old buddies!" Mr. Kessler said, pointing through the plate glass window at the front of the store. Just then the door opened, and in walked the Eagles' last two quarterbacks before this year—Matt Clayton and last year's QB, Cody Hansen.

"Yo, what's up?" Tiki called, and they all greeted one another with backslaps and team handshakes.

"What are you guys doing here?" Cody asked.

"Just taking a stroll down memory lane," said Tiki. "How's high school treating you?"

"Eh," Cody said, frowning. "Okay, I guess."

"He's just down because he's riding the bench this year," said Matt, putting an arm around Cody's shoulder. "Don't worry, dude. You'll get your shot. After I leave for college, that is."

"Not funny," said Cody.

"Actually, I got scouted for Randolph Prep for next season," Matt said.

"Wow, congratulations, man," Tiki said.

"That's awesome, Matt," Ronde added. Randolph Prep

was a football powerhouse. Kids from there went straight to places like Ole Miss, Alabama, and Notre Dame.

"So cheer up, dude," Matt told Cody. "You might be starting as soon as next year."

"Hmph," said Cody. "Not soon enough for me."

"Just chill, man," Ronde told him. "Matt's right. It won't be long till you're the man. Remember seventh grade? Tiki and I barely played that whole year."

"Not what I want to hear," said Cody.

Ronde knew how hard it must be for him. He'd gotten his chance to start in junior high early, when Matt broke his leg. So he'd never really suffered on the bench for very long, the way the rest of them had.

"I hope you're not wishing for me to get hurt again," Matt told Cody, only half-joking. They all knew what an intense competitor Cody was—not the most patient person in the world.

"The main thing is, you guys are winning," Ronde said. "You're 3–0, right? Hey, if you win the championship, it belongs to you as much as anyone else on the team, Cody."

"Skip it, Ronde. I've heard it all before," said Cody glumly.

"It's all about the team in the end," Ronde reminded him.

"Easy for you to say," said Cody. "You're the big star, and you play every down of every game."

"So far," Tiki pointed out.

"Stay positive, Cody," Ronde advised. "Remember last year. Remember what it took for us to win."

Cody gave him a long look, then nodded. "Ah, you're right, Ronde," he said, sighing. "I'm being kinda selfish, aren't I?"

"No, I wouldn't say that. . . ."

"I just said it for you," said Cody. "But that's over. It's not about me, like you said. It's all about the team."

Later, when they were getting up to go, Cody grabbed Ronde by the arm and said, "Thanks for that, man. I needed a reminder."

When they were outside again, Tiki looked at his twin in wonder. "Ronde, *you're* the one who should have the advice column."

"Oh, no, you don't," Ronde said, smiling and waving him off.

"Why not?" Tiki asked. "You're the one who's always got the good advice, not me."

"You're the one who won the essay contest, not me," Ronde shot back.

"Seriously, though," said Tiki. "How do you always know what to say to people? I mean like with Cody. That was impressive, dude. You really got him off his high horse."

Ronde shrugged. "I don't know," he said. "I figure most people already know what they should do to solve their problems. They just want somebody else to tell them they're right. That way they know they're just like everybody else, and not some kind of freak."

Tiki nodded slowly as they walked, letting Ronde's words sink in.

"Anyway," Ronde continued, "I've got no time for an advice column. I've got to concentrate on gaining some inches and pounds, not to mention As and Bs."

"I don't have time either," Tiki admitted. "I heard today that six letters came to the *Weekly Eagle* office for me to answer! Six! In one day! Can you imagine? What am I supposed to do, quit school and do this full-time?"

Ronde shook his head. "I forgot to mention, I especially need to concentrate on football—and so do *you*, Brother." He gave Tiki a meaningful look.

"What?" said Tiki, challenging him. "You got something on your mind, say it."

Ronde stopped walking and faced his twin. "Okay. You saw how distracted you got at practice, and this thing you're doing is just getting bigger and bigger. How're we supposed to win another championship if you're busy thinking about your newspaper column?"

Tiki didn't answer. He just looked at the ground, then started walking again.

Ronde followed him and caught up quickly. "Well?" he asked.

"I'm thinking," Tiki said, frowning, letting Ronde's

words sink in as they kept on walking into the sunset, headed for home.

The Eagles were 2–0, which, when you looked at it, was pretty good, considering they'd started 0–2 last year, and then come back to win it all. It made 2–0 look like a big improvement.

Still, Ronde thought, they'd been very lucky so far. Their first game had been against an easy opponent. Last week had been much tougher, and they'd nearly lost.

This week, against the Blue Ridge Bears, would be another tough test—the second of three away games in a row against last year's play-off teams. Next week it would be Pulaski, but Ronde didn't even want to think that far ahead. As tough as the Bears were, the Pulaski Wildcats were even tougher.

The Eagles were noisy and confident on the bus ride across town—*too* confident, in Ronde's humble opinion. He would have preferred a quiet bus, with every player inside his own head, collecting his thoughts, getting his mental game together.

Team spirit was fine, for what it was worth, but spirit alone wasn't going to beat the Bears today. They'd have to bring their "A" game, mentally as well as physically.

Coach Wheeler had prepared them well, as usual, showing lots of videos and drilling the team until the rookies looked and acted like veterans. But would they be able to keep it together under game conditions, especially if the Eagles fell behind early?

Sure enough, the game began badly. During the opening kickoff the Bears surprised the Eagles with an onside kick, which led to a fumble recovered by the kicking team. Two plays later the stunned Eagles were down 7–0.

During the ensuing kickoff, the team was prepared for another surprise, and it got one, although it wasn't an onside kick. Instead the Bears hit a squib kick, forcing one of the Eagles blockers to grab the ball. He barely hung on to it, and finally the offense got to work.

Luke Frazier was a good blocker, and he was getting better every week. He could carry the ball too, which allowed the Eagles to pull some surprise plays of their own, like the double reverse, and the handoff lateral pass. Coach Wheeler wasn't calling any of those plays early on, though. He wanted to see if his Eagles could move the ball against Blue Ridge.

They couldn't. Not even Tiki was able to break free from the powerful arms of the Blue Ridge linebackers. After two hard-won first downs, the Eagles were forced to punt the ball away.

The first quarter went quickly, with very few stops of the clock. Both teams were trying to advance on the ground and not take too many chances. But it was the Bears who were gaining more yards, winning the battle of field position. As the quarter came to an end, they were threatening again, third and goal on the Eagles seven.

The gun sounded, the whistle blew, and the teams trotted to the other end of the field to begin the new quarter. Ronde knew the Bears would be looking to the air on third down. With little room to maneuver, he guessed they'd shoot for the end zone. So he could lie back and wait for his man to approach, keeping his eyes on the quarterback in case he decided to roll out or run with the ball.

The ball was snapped, and Ronde kept his eyes squarely on the quarterback. Out of the corner of his eye, he saw his man make a move and head for the corner of the end zone. Knowing what would happen next, he sped off after him. He reached his man just as the ball did.

Ronde reached out and batted it away. But instead of it going out of bounds, the ball bounced off the top of the receiver's helmet and back in toward the end zone. Before it hit the ground, it was grabbed by one of the Bears' other receivers for a touchdown!

Ronde couldn't believe it. He'd made the play perfectly, and yet he'd cost his team a touchdown! An extra point later it was 14–0, and things were going even worse than they had gone the week before.

On the sidelines things were ominously quiet. Gone was the noise and the confidence the team had shown on the bus ride over. In its place was a gloomy hush, filled with dread and the smell of defeat.

What now? Ronde wondered how they could ever turn this around? And what else could the team do to play the way they could? The way they used to?

Okay, so they'd had a few unlucky breaks so far. But Blue Ridge seemed better prepared than the Eagles. They had obviously been thinking about this game, and about beating the Eagles, since last year's play-off game. The Bears were a team on a mission. How were the Eagles going to stop them, now that they were already in a deep, deep hole?

Late in the second quarter things got even worse. With the team behind by 14–0, Coach Wheeler had no choice but to take to the passing game. Manny Alvaro, now an eighth grader, was talented but still inexperienced. His two wide receivers were seventh graders, right out of elementary school with almost no game experience.

It was a recipe for disaster, and Ronde wished Coach would have stuck to the running game. Ronde was sure that if he'd done that the defense could have held the Bears scoreless the rest of the way, and the Eagles would still have had time to catch up.

But with Tiki going nowhere, and Luke showing his inexperience as a blocker, Wheeler obviously felt it was time to try something different.

Bad move. Manny overthrew Frank Amadou on a long bomb on first down. Then, after a screen pass to Tiki that was almost intercepted, Manny made a bad decision. Felix and Frank Amadou were supposed to do a crossing pattern. Frank, though, messed up his cut, and the two brothers wound up right next to each other, along with both cornerbacks and the free safety.

In spite of there being a crowd, Manny threw the ball straight into the traffic. It was batted around by at least three players before being intercepted by the safety and run back all the way to the Eagles twenty-two!

On the very next play, the Bears ran a quarterback option to the weak side. Ronde, all the way across the field, could only watch in disbelief as the quarterback leapt over two Eagles defenders and into the end zone for another score!

A loud groan went up from the Eagles bench. Ronde tore at his hair in frustration, but he couldn't take the time to dwell on the situation. It was his turn to take the kickoff. With only forty-five seconds left in the half, he took the kick, knowing that if the Eagles didn't score now, they'd be down by twenty-one points at the half.

Somehow he had to give his team a chance to put some points on the board!

After grabbing the ball out of the air, he sped straight downfield, sidestepping one, two, three defenders. They were left grabbing air while Ronde kept on running.

"Good things come in small packages," he kept telling himself as he dodged bigger, slower, clumsier players who could have crushed him if they'd been able to catch him. "Good things come in . . . small . . . packages."

He stutter-stepped his way past another of the Bears, and broke into open grass. There was the end zone, straight ahead of him. Nothing between him and it but—

"OOOF!" Somebody smacked into him just before he hit the goal line. Somebody he hadn't seen coming. Ronde hit the ground, and the ball went flying away from him.

"Nooooo!!" he cried in vain, as two huge, beefy Bears fell on the ball in their own end zone. An Eagles player touched them up for a safety. The Eagles were on the board, all right. Only instead of a seven-point touchdown, they'd scored only a two-point safety!

The gun sounded the end of the half with the Eagles trailing 21–2. The team headed into the locker room, and Ronde followed them, wondering whether his team had any fight left in them.

Ronde entered the visitors' locker room to find a downcast bunch of Eagles. His first instinct was to say something, but then he remembered what Tiki always said. You couldn't try the same tactic time after time and expect it to keep working the same way.

"Come on, you guys," Ronde urged. "Don't give up now. We've got thirty minutes of playing time left!"

A few heads looked up at him, a few pairs of eyes with almost no hope left in them. Over in the corner Coach Wheeler stood leaning against a locker, arms folded over his chest, waiting to see what his captains had to say before taking the floor himself.

Ronde looked at Tiki, waiting for him to say something. He was the famous public speaker, after all. He couldn't just expect his twin to do all the talking when the game was on the line.

Tiki looked around the room slowly. "You guys look like a pack of beaten dogs," he said. "Well, I don't know about you, but I'm not beaten. Ronde, are you beaten?"

"Nuh-uh, not me," Ronde said quickly.

"Let me tell you something," Tiki continued, "and you seventh graders listen up especially. We're gonna win this game, okay? I guarantee it."

Everyone was listening now. Tiki's sudden—and to Ronde's thinking, reckless—guarantee had gotten their total attention.

"We've got a bunch of veterans on this team who know how to play the game and who know how to win. Right, Paco?"

"That's right!" Paco said, with a look of fierce determination on his chubby face.

"We've come from behind before. Well, maybe not this far behind, but so what? Who wants to stand up and tell me we can't do it?"

He looked around the room. The other Eagles were looking around too, waiting to see if anyone wanted to argue with Tiki.

No one did. "Good," said Tiki. "I guess you all agree with me, then." He waited. Silence. "Well? Do you agree with me? Are we gonna get up off the floor and beat these guys?"

"Yeah!" said several of the Eagles.

"I hear something, but I can't make it out," Tiki said, cupping his ear.

"YEAH!!" everyone shouted.

Tiki nodded slowly. "That's what I thought. When that gun sounds, I want to see every one of us ready to play." He looked over at Coach Wheeler. "Coach? It's all yours."

Wheeler smiled. "You heard it, gentlemen. A victory has been guaranteed. Are you all gonna make a liar out of Tiki?"

"NO!!" everyone roared.

"Are we gonna win this game?"

"YEAH!"

Wheeler clapped his hands. "Okay, then. No more of those gloomy faces. Let's all think about how we're gonna play our game. Veterans, this game is on your shoulders. Rookies, just relax and follow the veterans' lead. Be ready for the ball to bounce your way—because it will, just when you least expect it. Be opportunists, and let's make every break count!"

As they made their way back onto the field, Ronde glanced over at Tiki, who was unusually quiet and intense.

He sure hoped Tiki was right and they wound up winning. Because if they lost after that guarantee of his, Tiki was going to look like a total loser.

Down by nineteen points, the Eagles had to start out on defense. With their big lead the Bears just kept the ball on the ground, eating up as much clock as they could, and keeping the ball out of the hands of the Eagles offense, especially Tiki Barber.

Ronde was getting frustrated. Why didn't they ever throw the ball to Ronde's man and give Ronde a chance to make a play? He couldn't even blitz and sack the quarterback if the Bears were just going to run it every play!

He could only hope that the Eagles' defensive line and linebackers could hold against the relentless Blue Ridge ground attack. Rob Fiorilla, Sam Scarfone's replacement, was big, strong, and fast, but until now he hadn't shown a nose for the ball—that instinct you got from playing a lot, that told you where the runner was going to be heading.

Now, though, he seemed to be learning fast. On two plays in a row he stuffed the run, stopping it cold. That brought up a third and nine at midfield. Ronde smiled, rubbing his hands together. This was his chance. On third and long the Bears would have to pass.

Coach sent in the play—a safety blitz. That meant that Ronde would have to dog his man, staying close to him while the safety made a run for the quarterback. If the safety failed to get to the quarterback, Ronde would be alone on his man, with no help.

Well, that was fine with him. He was as ready as he'd ever be. He stared across at his man—a tall, rangy boy with long, powerful legs. Ronde'd been able to stay with him all day, though, because the kid's moves weren't all that great.

Now Ronde gave him a hard bump coming off the line, so that the kid was in no shape to receive the pass. Ronde looked over to see the quarterback scrambling away from the blitzing safety.

Ronde's man was getting up now, signaling for the pass to come his way. The quarterback saw him, and Ronde did too. Diving in front of the receiver, Ronde snatched the pass out of thin air and held on to it for the interception!

It was the break the Eagles desperately needed. Now the offense took over, with Tiki shouldering the load. He slashed right through the Bears defensive line like a hot knife through butter, eating up yards by the dozen. In no time at all the Eagles were knocking at the door.

Manny took the snap at the three, and tossed it quickly and softly over the heads of the defenders, and into the waiting arms of Frank Amadou. Touchdown, Eagles!

On their next offensive series of downs, the Bears kept to the ground again, still using the same strategy. Only this time the Eagles were ready for it. They loaded up their linebackers to stuff the run, and after a couple of first downs, they were able to force another third and long situation.

This time the Bears threw to the side of the field farthest from Ronde, avoiding him. They connected for a

first down and were able to use up most of the third quarter before the Eagles defense finally held firm and forced
a long field goal attempt, which missed.

The Eagles offense now started to mix in some quick
passes. Some to Tiki, a couple to Justin, and one bullet to Felix Amadou that set the Eagles up at the Bears
twenty. That's when Coach Wheeler called for the Statue
of Liberty play.

It was a trick play, one they'd practiced since last year
but had used only once. On the snap, Manny dropped
back to pass, held his arm back—and Tiki grabbed the
ball from him, running around the end. Before the
defense knew what had happened, Tiki had turned the
corner and was heading for pay dirt!

Only a last-minute tackle stopped him short of the
goal line, but they scored on the next play anyway, just
in time for the end of the third quarter.

They switched ends of the field and kicked off to the
Bears. Ronde flew down the field and was about to pile
into the ballcarrier when he was blocked in the back
and taken down. He got up yelling, trying to get the ref's
attention. "That was a penalty!" he screamed, but it was
no use. The refs were not watching. Their eyes were
downfield, where the Blue Ridge return man was scam-
pering all the way into the end zone!

"NOOO!!!" Ronde moaned, grabbing his helmet with
both hands. An extra point later it was 28–16, Bears.

"Never mind!" he yelled at the stunned Eagles players as he got back to the sideline. "We're still going to win this one! Stay focused! The ball's gonna bounce our way. Just be ready for that one big break!"

He clapped his hands with all his might, and some of the players started nodding and agreeing with him, clapping their hands along with his.

Seeing that they were going to be okay, Ronde ran back onto the field to receive the kickoff. He got the ball up to midfield and then turned it over to Tiki and the offense. "Let's go!" he shouted to his brother.

"Don't worry. I got this," Tiki assured him, saluting.

And he did. Only not in the way he might have thought. The Eagles were still in passing mode, with Coach Wheeler trying to make up ground quickly. But Frank Amadou, after making a spectacular grab, tried to turn it into a long gain. The safety blindsided him, knocking the ball free—and right into Tiki's hands.

Ronde could see that his twin was surprised, but only for an instant. It was the lucky bounce they'd both been talking about, and Tiki ran with it, all the way to the end zone!

Back within five points after Adam's extra point, the Eagles kicked off again. Time was getting short— just three minutes left—and the Bears weren't about to change their strategy. As long as they had the ball, they were going to try to kill off the minutes and seconds by running it every play.

Only on third down plays would they go to the air, and only if they needed more than five yards for a first down. Ronde batted down one of those passes, but the Bears went for it on fourth down and got the yardage they needed.

However, on the next third-down play, Ronde got the call he wanted from the coach—a blitz—and he laid a solid hit on the quarterback for a crucial sack!

The Bears missed another long field goal attempt, and the ball went back to the Eagles. Time for one last drive before the clock ran out.

Tiki took the handoff on the first three Eagles plays, and each time, he ran for a first down. Now the team was in Bears territory, but the Eagles, out of time-outs, had to throw to the sidelines to stop the clock.

And that's when disaster nearly struck. On a square-out pattern Justin Landzberg grabbed the ball, only to lose it when he got hit by the safety, who came flying through the air to knock the ball loose.

It fell into the hands of the Bears cornerback for the interception. And if he had only gone down to the turf, that would have been the end of everything for the Eagles. Their hopes for an undefeated season, along with Tiki's rash guarantee, would have been dashed to pieces.

But the Bears player who'd come down with the ball tried to run with it. Maybe he saw open field in front of him. Maybe he had dreams of scoring a glorious touch-down to beat the Eagles. Maybe he just wasn't thinking.

Whatever it was, he tried to run, and that gave Tiki the chance to go after him. Catching him at midfield, he reached out and stripped the ball. Not only did he pry it free, but he snatched it out of the guy's hands in midstride!

Not finished yet, Tiki turned back toward the Bears' end zone. Everyone was rushing at him from all directions, but somehow he kept his feet, working himself free of every would-be tackler, until he was finally brought down at the three yard line!

The Eagles quickly lined up so that Manny could spike the ball. Four seconds left—time for only one more play. Coach Wheeler sent the play in from the sidelines— play action for Tiki.

Winded but happy, Tiki lined up. He'd given it his all, but he had enough left for just one more play. . . .

Manny faked the handoff to him, then spun around the other way, looking into the end zone. Then, not finding anyone open, he turned back to Tiki and fired it to him right on the goal line. Tiki sank to his knees, sticking out his arms with the ball so that there would be no doubt.

TOUCHDOWN!

The gun sounded. The game was over. The greatest comeback in Eagles' history—or at least in recent memory—was complete. And Tiki had made good on his guarantee of victory!

Ronde felt a rush of happiness and relief come over

him as he ran onto the field to join in the happy pileup of Eagles.

And yet, even as they jumped for joy and chanted their victory chant, Ronde knew that this incredible game was only one baby step on the way toward their ultimate goal.

Next week would bring them an even tougher opponent—the Pulaski Wildcats, who'd come in first in the league last year and were even stronger this year. Would the Eagles feed on this comeback over the Bears to come together as a great team? Or would this be the high-water mark of their season?

# CHAPTER TEN

## OUT OF FOCUS

TIKI HAD TO ADMIT, IT WAS GREAT BEING
everybody's hero. Everyone wanted to be his friend,
everyone loved him, thought all his jokes were funny,
thought he was the coolest thing since the air condi-
tioner had been invented. They wanted his autograph,
his advice, his company.

Only problem was, there wasn't enough of Tiki to go
around. He felt like a cake that everyone wanted a piece
of and was grabbing at until there were only stale crumbs
left to eat.

On Sunday at five o'clock he remembered he had
a big math test the next morning. He hadn't even had
time to study! He tore himself away from the TV, where
Ronde was watching the Chicago Bears shellacking the
Washington Redskins.

"Where you going?" Ronde called after him.

"Gotta study," Tiki said.

"Oh. I already did mine."

"Yeah, good for you. Enjoy the game."

"I will. Oh, and don't forget your advice column.

Didn't Laura say she wanted it by tomorrow?"

"Dang!" Tiki said, wincing as it all came back to him. "I forgot about that, too. I've got eighty-four letters to read through!"

"You don't have to read them all, do you?" Ronde asked, dumbfounded.

"How would you feel if you had a problem and sent a letter and the advice guy didn't even read it?" Tiki pointed out.

"I guess you're right. Oh, well. See you around bedtime, 'cause you won't be taking time out for supper." Ronde laughed, grabbed a big bag of potato chips, and started stuffing his face. "Yesshhh!" he shouted at the TV as Walter Payton broke a big run for the Bears, smashing through the Redskins defense. "Tiki, look. It's your main man!"

"Yeah, whatever," Tiki said, frowning. "I've gotta go get busy."

He studied math for a while, but it was hard to concentrate with that big pile of letters staring him in the face. After about twenty minutes he gave up and started reading them.

As he went through each one, he took notes on a pad and drafted a quick response. Most of them were easy problems, things he'd been through before himself and had found a way out of. The few that were more difficult he put aside for later.

He wrote up the easy responses neatly and put them in a pile. These he'd give to Laura so that she could hand them to the questioners. They would not be featured in the column, which had room for only one response per week.

There were three tougher questions. Tiki spent a good amount of time on each of them and carefully thought out how he would go about solving their problem if he were them.

One of the three was the most interesting, and that was the last one he dealt with. This response would be his column for the week.

Dear Confused,

It's not unusual to like someone who doesn't like you back. Just remember that famous American saying "Time heals all wounds." Sooner or later, you'll stop liking that person and start liking somebody else. And remember, the person you like may like you too, only not the same kind of like. I know you know what I'm talking about. Just hang in there, and try not to think too much about it. Above all, don't get down on yourself. There are probably people out there who like you that way, and you don't even know it!

There. That was done. Not that he knew much about the subject. His life was too busy right now for stuff like that. Still, it was interesting, trying to get into Confused's head and heart, and feel their feelings along with them.

He put his pen down, rubbed his eyes, and realized it was nine o'clock. He hadn't even eaten dinner! No one had called him to the table. Tiki knew that was because Ronde had explained the situation to their mom. But now he was starving. He ran downstairs, to find his dinner on the table, nicely covered with a pot lid.

"Mac and cheese!" he cried as he lifted the lid. "My favorite!"

"It's cold, baby," his mom said. "It's been sitting there like that for an hour and a half!"

"Sorry, Ma."

"My, my, you've been working hard," she said, stroking the top of his head. "Your brain must be all worn out from studying."

Tiki was about to tell her he'd spent only twenty minutes studying and the rest of the time reading and writing letters, but he thought better of it. He knew what she'd say: "Study first, and spend time on your hobbies later." By "hobbies," she usually meant "football." But a column for the school paper would also qualify in her book as less important than studying for a big math test, and he knew it.

He only hoped he got an A, or at least a B. And hope was about all he had left, since he'd gone through the work so fast it hadn't stuck in his mind at all!

Tiki left math class that Monday feeling weird but good. He'd done okay on the test. At least he thought he had.

After his last class of the day, he headed over to the *Weekly Eagle* office to hand in his column and his responses to the letters he'd gotten.

Laura was waiting for him. "Right on time!" she chirped, taking the papers from him and handing him a big stack. "Here. These are for next week."

"Huh?"

"Twenty-three letters this time. Your second column comes out Wednesday, and already it's a big hit! Congrats, Tiki. When you're a famous reporter, remember who gave you your start."

It took him a second to realize she was kidding. Then he gave her a weak laugh, took the letters, stuffed them into his book bag, and headed on out of there. If things kept on going like this, by October he'd have thirty letters a week to answer!

He had to get to practice quick, or he'd be late. But as he was about to open the stairway door, he heard his name being called. Turning, he saw Cootie, the Eagles' mascot, running toward him, waving.

"Wait up, Tiki!" he said. "Got a minute?"

"Uh, not really," Tiki told him. "I've gotta get to practice."

"Oh. Yeah. Sure . . ." Cootie seemed unsure of what to say. Clearly he was upset about something. Tiki could see that from the way his eyes were darting this way and that.

"Something on your mind, Cootie?"

"Yeah. . . . Can we talk in private?" Cootie indicated the stairs, which were empty now that school had let out.

"Okay, sure," Tiki said, "but try to make it quick."

"Right, right," said Cootie, waiting till the door swung closed behind them. "It's . . . Well, it's about the costume."

"The costume? What's wrong with it?"

"Nothing . . . and everything. I was going to write you a letter about it, but I knew that if you answered it in your column, everyone would know the letter was from me. Because of the costume and all."

"I get it," Tiki said. "So, what's the problem with it?"

"The problem is, people don't treat me like just another kid," said Cootie. "They treat me like I'm Ernie the Eagle, you know? Like, they don't take me seriously. I'm a joke to them."

"Wow." Tiki nodded, imagining what it must be like to be Ernie the Eagle instead of yourself. Ernie was kind of a cartoon Eagle, so it was easy to see how kids would consider Cootie a less-than-serious person. "I get what you're saying."

"Well?" Cootie asked. "What can I do about it? I don't want to quit—not when the Eagles are undefeated. But it's getting to be too much for me to take . . . and I just thought, well, you being an advice columnist and all . . ."

"Sure, sure, Cootie," Tiki told him. "Only I've got to get to practice. Let me think on it, okay?"

"But don't write about it in the paper!" Cootie pleaded. "It's got to stay private—between us."

"Sure thing."

"I mean, you can't tell anyone. Not even Ronde."

"Huh?"

"If he finds out, the whole team is gonna know."

"Hmm, you've got a point," said Tiki. Ronde wasn't a big talker, except among his Eagles teammates. With them, though, he could be a regular motormouth, and no one's secrets were safe when that happened. "Okay, I won't tell him."

"You can't even tell your mom!" Cootie said, clutching Tiki's shirtsleeve.

"My mom? Why not?"

"She knows my mom," Cootie reminded him. "From the office."

Tiki nodded. Cootie's mom and his own were employees at the same place, and had known each other for years.

"You got it, man. It's just between us. Look, I've gotta book. See you soon, okay?"

"Wait!"

Tiki froze on the steps. *What now?* he wondered. "Yeah?"

Cootie paused. "Nothing. Just . . . thanks. Thanks for being my friend."

Tiki blinked. "Yeah. Sure thing. No problem."

He continued down the stairs, but he could still

feel Cootie's eyes on him. Was he Cootie's friend? Not really—only in the sense that he was everybody's friend, especially anyone associated with the Eagles. But he was obviously somebody very important to Cootie, and his advice meant a lot to him. He would have to think of a solution to Cootie's problem, but right now he had bigger fish to fry.

He got to the locker room fifteen minutes late. Most of the other players were already out on the field, practicing. A few were still inside, watching a video of the Pulaski Wildcats with Coach Wheeler.

"Tiki!" the coach greeted him, pausing the video. "So good of you to grace us with your presence."

Tiki flashed a shy grin. "Sorry," he told them all. "I had to stop at the newspaper office and drop off my column for the week. And then . . . well, this kid had a problem and needed to talk to me. . . ."

He expected Coach to leave it at that, but instead Wheeler told the other kids to head on out to the field, saying he wanted to talk to Tiki for a minute privately.

*Uh-oh,* thought Tiki. *What now?* Didn't he already have enough on his mind?

"I can't remember the last time you were late for a practice," Coach began, sitting on the bench next to Tiki and watching him strap on his protective gear. "Is there a problem I should be aware of?"

"No, no, Coach. I'm fine," Tiki assured him.

"I hope so," Wheeler said. "Because I've got to say, you seem quite distracted these days."

Tiki stopped strapping on the gear. A feeling of dread was gripping his insides. "I do?"

"Getting hit in the head with the football, showing up late for practice . . . Is it just me? Or is there something going on in your life that I need to know about?"

"No, everything's great," Tiki said. "It's just . . ."

"Yeeesss?"

Tiki sighed. "I've just got a lot of responsibilities, is all."

Coach nodded. "I thought it might be something like that. You know, Tiki, you do have a lot of responsibility. The younger kids on the team all look up to you. And of course you and Ronde did so much last year to win us a championship. This year everybody's expecting even more out of you."

"I'm fine with all that," Tiki said. "I mean—I'm fine, Coach. No problem."

"You're sure?"

"Sure."

"You're sure it's not because of *this*?" Coach Wheeler reached into his back pocket and pulled out a copy of the *Weekly Eagle*, with the "Dear Tiki" page showing.

"Oh," Tiki said, seeing it. "Oh . . . that."

"It must have taken a lot of work."

"You have no idea," Tiki said, managing a laugh.

"It's very good, by the way. I thought your advice was very thoughtful."

"Thanks," Tiki said. Then, "But?"

"But is this going to go on the whole football season? Because I'll be honest with you, I think it's taking its toll on my star halfback."

"No, Coach. I can handle it," Tiki insisted.

Wheeler smiled sadly. "Schoolwork too?"

"I can handle it," Tiki repeated, leaving no more room for doubt.

"All right, then," Coach finally said, giving up. "Go on out and practice. But I hope we won't have to talk about this again."

"We won't," Tiki promised, and got out of there as fast as he could.

Coach Wheeler's words bothered him greatly. It wasn't that he had said anything Tiki hadn't already told himself. It's just that it was different coming from your head coach, the man you turned to for advice more than anyone except . . .

*Hmmm,* thought Tiki. *Maybe I should ask her.*

*PLUNK!!*

Again, incredibly, the football hit him right in the helmet. Manny, who had thrown the ball, started laughing hysterically. "Tiki's in dreamland again!" he said, pointing.

"Yoo-hoo," Paco chimed in. "Lassie, come home!"

Everyone was laughing now. Everyone but Tiki. He was thinking of Cootie, and how people must laugh at him all the time. This was how it felt. He told himself to remember the feeling. Hopefully it would help him come up with an answer for Cootie's problem.

As for himself, Tiki decided to just ignore the laughter. When game time came against Pulaski, he would show them all that he could handle it—the game, the column, his schoolwork, being the big man on campus. Everything.

For now he just kept repeating the mantra that had gotten him this far: Play proud. He was a dynamo for the rest of practice, and nobody laughed when he slammed into them carrying the football.

Nobody.

Still he wondered if it was nothing more than a slogan, if his confidence was just an act to fool everyone else. He remembered when Ronde wondered the same thing about him. He remembered his twin's words of advice too. *Most people already know what they should do.*

Could he really handle it all, and do his best at everything?

"Yes," he muttered under his breath. "I can, because I have to. Everyone is counting on me, and I can't let them down."

If the truth was that he couldn't handle it all, that he wasn't as perfect as everyone thought he was—well, he wasn't ready to admit that. Not yet. Not even to himself.

• • •

Tiki tried to stay ahead of things that week. He spent every second of study hall doing homework, so that when he got home after practice he'd have time to answer all those letters asking for his advice.

He answered the easy ones first, just like the week before. Then he tackled the three or four that were the most challenging. From these he picked the one that he wanted to use for next week's column. By the time he'd finished, it was nine thirty again. Time for dessert and bed, and nothing else.

This couldn't go on—not for the rest of the school year, or the rest of the football season. He hadn't had a second to himself, just to relax, since Ms. Adair had handed out the form for that stupid essay contest.

No, it wasn't stupid, he admitted to himself. In another world, where he wasn't the star of the football team, it might have been a fantastic opportunity for him.

But the way things were?

Tiki felt like he was about to burst from all the pressure that was being put on him.

He washed up, brushed his teeth, and got into bed. Ronde was already snoring. It didn't take him long, Tiki thought with a pang of jealousy. All Ronde had to worry about was hitting his growth spurt. Nothing to keep him awake at night.

And then Tiki remembered—he hadn't thought of a

solution to Cootie's problem! Oh, no. Now he'd never get to sleep!

What could he tell the poor kid?

The game against Pulaski came up so fast that Tiki almost didn't see it coming. Was it really Friday already? Had the whole week gone by without him noticing the passing of the days?

He'd been to practice twice, although he hadn't done very well. He could see the looks Coach Wheeler kept giving him, and he knew what they meant. Coach had not been convinced by Tiki's statement that he could handle three things at once—football, schoolwork, and his job at the school paper.

That job had gotten much bigger. If he was honest with himself, Tiki had to admit that it was other kids' troubles that had occupied most of the time, attention, and space in his brain these past two weeks.

Although he still hadn't figured out an answer to Cootie's problem, he *had* gotten all twenty-three advice letters answered, and he'd picked the one he thought was best for his second column. He left the rest of his responses in a box at the *Weekly Eagle*, for private pickup by Anxious, Nerdy, Clueless, and all the other kids who'd written him under made-up names, hoping for an answer to their problems.

This week Tiki had also taken his math and English

unit tests. Ouch. Tiki bit his lip as he remembered how blindsided he'd been by his grades—B minus in English, and C in math!

His mom had not been pleased. "What is this you're handing me?" she'd asked him, her eyes burning right through him. "This is not *my* son's test. This is some other mother's son's test. My son doesn't bring home Cs and B minuses. He takes his education seriously."

"*I* take *my* education seriously," Ronde had piped up.

"Be quiet, Ronde," their mom had said. "You got very nice grades, but I'm talking to your brother now."

"Yes, ma'am."

Tiki had shot Ronde an annoyed look, and then had turned to face his mom.

"Do you have an explanation for me?" she'd asked.

He'd shrugged. "I guess I didn't study hard enough."

"How much time did you give to each subject?"

He'd shrugged again. "I didn't count."

"Well, you'd better devote more time from now on. I don't want to see these kinds of grades again. Ever. Do you understand?"

"Yes, ma'am." And that had been the end of it, at least for that evening. But he had studied for both those tests. The trouble was, he'd kept getting distracted, finding himself drawn into those tricky problems so many of his fellow students seemed to be grappling with!

Tiki knew in his heart that Coach Wheeler and Ronde

were right. Agreeing to do the advice column had been a mistake. But what could he do now? So many kids were depending on him.

And now here it was, Friday afternoon, and they were riding the bus for their third straight road game, into the jaws of the hated, dreaded Pulaski Wildcats.

# CHAPTER ELEVEN

## ANSWERING THE CALL

*FOR THE PAST MONTH RONDE HAD BEEN BRISTLING* over the fact that Tiki was bigger than him. Not just taller, or stronger, or having bigger muscles, or getting all the attention because as a running back he scored more touchdowns than Ronde. No, it wasn't just that. It was also his winning the essay contest when Ronde had gotten only an honorable mention. And it was Tiki's getting offered the advice column when it was he, Ronde, who always had the best advice to give.

Yes, okay, he admitted it. He was jealous of his twin. But the worst part was when the Eagles themselves started buying into it. "We can't lose!" the younger players would keep saying. "We've got Tiki!" Not "We've got the Barber twins," but "We've got Tiki." He loved his brother, of course—and he wished him well, but not more well than he wished himself!

It made Ronde's blood boil. But it also made him worry about Tiki. His twin had been in a haze all week. It had started with that stupid essay contest, and things had only gotten worse since he'd started writing that advice column. Tiki had never come home with such bad grades before. Even Ronde was shocked. If Tiki wasn't paying attention to his schoolwork, how was he going to give football everything he had?

For the past two weeks the Eagles had come from behind after playing ugly most of the game. They'd gotten lucky both times. But expecting lightning to strike three times in the same place was a recipe for getting shocked. The Pulaski Wildcats were not just good. They'd finished in first place the year before, and they were almost all returning ninth graders. They were deep, experienced, and loaded for bear. Everyone—especially Pulaski—wanted revenge on the Eagles.

If the Eagles had an ugly start today, things could go south in a hurry. And if Tiki played at less than his best, it would take the air right out of the Eagles' balloon. All those "We can't lose, we've got Tiki" chants. What would those kids think if Tiki choked in the clutch?

He'd been awful in practice all week, but that didn't seem to bother anybody else except Ronde and Coach Wheeler. Everyone else, including Tiki, kept brushing it off, saying it was only practice.

That wasn't the way to win, and Ronde and Coach both knew it. Tiki used to know it too. What had happened to him?

Ronde thought he knew. He'd tried talking to Tiki, but his twin was too proud to change his mind.

Well, there was nothing Ronde could do about it now. If Tiki wasn't going to bring his "A" game, that was out of Ronde's hands.

What he could control was his *own* performance, he realized. "Good things come in small packages," he reminded himself, grinning as he remembered the subject of his honorable-mention-winning essay.

"Game on!" he shouted as he and Tiki led the team out of the tunnel and onto the field. They were greeted by a chorus of boos from the stands packed with Pulaski fans. *Not exactly polite*, thought Ronde. But hey, when you're state champs, the also-rans are not going to give you a lot of love.

The Eagles received the kickoff, with Ronde getting tackled at the forty yard line. Their first drive featured Manny going to the air. They managed to get off a few completions because the Wildcats had been expecting to see a lot of Tiki, a star they knew from last year. Instead Coach Wheeler threw them a curveball, and it resulted in a field goal for the Eagles.

But Pulaski had come to play on offense. By running on virtually every play, they steered clear of Ronde. Their well-executed blocks created lots of space for the halfback and fullback, and before long Pulaski had a 7–3 lead.

On their next three drives, the Eagles went with their ground game. Tiki wasn't making much progress, though.

Every time he tried to find a hole, it was quickly closed and he had to settle for short yardage. The Eagles did manage one more field goal before the half, but that was all.

Pulaski, however, was unstoppable. They scored two more touchdowns before the half, and were driving again when the gun sounded. The Eagles staggered into the locker room, down 21–6 and showing no signs of life.

Coach Wheeler lit into the linemen first. "You've got to hold your lanes!" he shouted. "Hit 'em low, and quit grabbing. Those penalties are killing us! And, Tiki, if you don't see daylight, you've got to rethink the play, understand? You can't keep hitting your head against a brick wall and expect it to give way!"

Tiki nodded, staring at the floor between his legs.

"I thought we went over this in the video," Wheeler said, still focused on Tiki. "Their middle linebacker, he's the one to keep your eye on. When he cuts one way, you cut the other. Don't you remember? Or weren't you paying attention?"

Tiki shrugged. To Ronde it looked like his twin was ready to cry. Wheeler must have sensed it too, because he backed off.

"Use your head, Tiki, like you usually do. We need you out there, giving it everything you've got. Understand?"

Tiki nodded again, but his head stayed down. The locker room was dead silent. Their captain on offense had just gotten a dressing-down from the coach! Their invincible hero had just been humbled.

"Okay, listen up. They get the ball first next half," Wheeler went on. "Defense, I want you thinking about stripping the ball. We've got to create some mistakes and throw them off their game a little. Right now they've got all the momentum. I want each of you to think about how you're going to be the one to make the play that swings the game around! Now get back out there, Eagles, and show them what you're made of!"

They went back out, but many of them didn't look convinced by Coach Wheeler's speech.

Ronde, for his part, had taken Coach's words to heart. "It's gonna be me," he told himself. "Good things come in small packages. Good things come in small packages."

He flew down the field after the kickoff, and upended the runner so fiercely that he tumbled head over heels, hitting the ground so hard that the ball came loose! An Eagles player fell onto it for the recovery, and Coach Wheeler had the big momentum-shifting play he'd asked for!

"How'd you do that, Bro?" Tiki asked, grinning.

Ronde stared back at him without smiling. "Good things come in small packages, dude. He never saw me coming."

Tiki's jaw dropped. "That's it!" he cried.

"That's what?"

141

"N-never mind," Tiki said, waving him off. "Gotta get out there."

Ronde sat on the bench and watched to see if the momentum of the game really had shifted.

It had. Tiki took the ball on first down and made two quick cuts that left him free in the flat. Deking and spinning, he fought forward for eighteen yards and a first down!

In no time the Eagles were at the gates, first and goal at the seven. Tiki took the ball from Manny and ran behind Justin toward the corner. Just before getting there, Tiki cut straight back and downfield, finding a seam that hadn't been there a moment before, and leaving the Wildcats' star middle linebacker flat on his face in the grass!

On the next Pulaski drive Ronde lined up right on the line of scrimmage. Every play, he knocked his man out of the action with ferocious hits. Rob Fiorilla stuffed two runs that came his way, getting there before the ballcarrier to stuff the hole. On third down Ronde blitzed and grabbed the runner as he tried to go by him, throwing him for a loss. The Wildcats were forced to punt, and Ronde returned it all the way to the Pulaski twenty-five.

Tiki took it from there, grabbing a screen pass and following his blocking down to the seven. From there, Manny found Luke Frazier in the end zone, and the Pulaski lead was down to one point—21–20!

The fourth quarter began with a Wildcats drive that

ended up with a long field goal, extending the lead to 24–20. On their next three drives, the Eagles ate up a lot of ground, but they also ate up a lot of clock, and did not manage to score. The Wildcats, too, ate up the clock with their running game, which had just enough power to keep possession of the ball. On this hot day in early October, the Eagles defense, which had been on the field most of the game, was starting to wilt.

Finally the Eagles held on a big fourth-down play and took over at their own thirty-five with two minutes and twenty seconds left in the game.

Manny went to the air. Scrambling away from the blitzing Wildcats defense, he found Frank Amadou for twenty-five yards, then Luke Frazier for another ten. Now, at the Pulaski thirty, Coach Wheeler called Tiki's number for a quick dump pass in the flat.

They had one time-out left, so if he was tackled in the middle of the field, they could still stop the clock and have time for a few more plays. If he missed it, the clock would stop on the incompletion and it would still only be second down.

Tiki grabbed the pass, and deked his way for a first down. But instead of just going down, he decided to go for the kill right then. He fought like crazy for a few extra yards, staying up while more and more Wildcats defenders hit him.

It was a bad decision. One of those defenders grabbed

the ball and stripped it out of Tiki's hands! It flew into the air and was grabbed by another Pulaski player, who dropped to the ground with it, ending the play.

It was over!

Or was it? Ronde looked up at the clock. One minute forty seconds left, and they had only one time-out. They called it on first down. On second down the Wildcats quarterback took a knee. Ronde wondered if he'd do the same on third down. If he did, the clock would count down to almost nothing. Pulaski would have to punt, but if Ronde couldn't run it back for a touchdown, the Eagles would lose, because there would be no time left to run a play!

Yes, the Wildcats might play it that way, but Ronde thought not. They didn't want to put the game in his hands, because Ronde Barber had beaten them before. He thought they'd try to run the ball for a first down, rather than take a knee for the third time.

He didn't even bother to cover his man. He knew they wouldn't be thinking pass, because an incomplete pass would stop the clock, and they wanted it to run out.

He was right. Leaving his man alone, he darted into the backfield and hit the ballcarrier from behind just as he took the handoff. The ball flew from his hands, and into the waiting arms of Rob Fiorilla.

Ronde saw his eyes widen in surprise. Rob was not used to having the ball in his hands, and he obviously didn't know what to do with it.

"HERE!!" Ronde shouted, waving his arms wildly.

Rob came to just in time, and lateraled the ball to Ronde just as two Wildcats linemen slammed into him.

Ronde took the toss and was off to the races. Taller players with longer strides came after him, but none of them could catch him. Ronde never stopped until he'd run past the end zone and jumped into the padded wall separating the field from the bleachers.

Game over! Eagles 26, Pulaski 24!

Ronde had done it. He'd answered Coach Wheeler's challenge to be the one who changed the big game. He'd grabbed it just before it had gotten out of reach, and he'd snatched it back for his team. Now his teammates carried him off the field. He was their hero, at least for today.

He, not Tiki. The little guy had come through. And they'd never seen him coming.

# CHAPTER TWELVE

## THE ULTIMATE GOAL

**TIKI WAS AS THRILLED BY THE VICTORY AS ANY** of them—those wildly cheering, noisy, raucous boys on the bus back to Hidden Valley. It was a great win for the team, over their biggest local rival. It ended a string of three straight away games against last year's play-off opponents. Coming up was a string of five straight games against weaker competition that the Eagles could reasonably expect to win, if they didn't totally mess up.

By the time they met the Bears, Wildcats, and Rockets again, it would be the last three games of the season, and they would all be in the friendly confines of Hidden Valley field. The Eagles rookies would have had more than half a season's worth of experience. The team would be running on all cylinders, a well-oiled machine with lots of momentum. They would have every chance in the world at going undefeated.

The team's future was rosy, and all the Eagles knew it. What had been dangerous overconfidence was now easy, well-earned faith in themselves.

Still, inside, down deep inside where the others

couldn't see, Tiki was uneasy. He knew in his heart of hearts that he hadn't played his best, that his mistakes during the game and his lack of focus in practice had nearly cost the Eagles this latest of their three straight wins. The undefeated season of their dreams would have been gone forever, and their hopes for a state championship would have been seriously damaged.

Yes, they'd all been lucky. Tiki most of all. *Good old Ronde,* thought Tiki. *Without him we'd never have pulled it off these past three weeks.* Definitely Ronde had been the team MVP so far.

Tiki was sorry now he'd given his twin such a hard time over the growth spurt thing. Ronde didn't need to be big to make a difference in a football game—or in life, either. And of course he would catch up eventually, Tiki knew that. It was inevitable.

They got off the team bus and were driven home by Paco's mom, who dropped them off on her way. "Great going, you guys!" she called out her window as she waved good-bye.

"Go, Eagles!" the twins both shouted after her.

"Go, Eaaagllles," came Paco's retreating reply as the car drove away.

The boys stared at their house. It was dark. Their mom worked late on Friday evenings at her second job. Dinner would be in the oven, ready for heating up. Tiki wished she didn't have to work so hard. Then she could come to more of their games, like she used to when she had only the one job.

"Life is expensive," she always said. "Got to pay those bills if we expect to get along."

He was glad they had good news for her tonight. It always made her happy when the Eagles won, and when her boys played well.

"You were right, Ronde," Tiki said as they opened the door and went inside.

"About what?"

"About good things coming in small packages."

"Oh. That. Yeah, well . . ."

"You won us that game, Ronde. Without you we might be 1–3 right now."

Ronde shrugged it off. "Yeah, I guess." He went and took their dinners out of the oven. "Mac and cheese!" he said, breaking into a wide grin. It was their all-time favorite, and they got it about twice a week.

"Listen, I know I didn't do that great today,"

"I didn't say that," Ronde pointed out.

"You didn't have to," Tiki said. "I know when I'm playing proud and when I'm not."

"I guess it's easier to say it than to do it," Ronde said, turning the oven on to heat up their food.

"You got that right." Tiki went to the fridge. "What're you drinking?"

"We got grape juice?"

"Grape or orange, or else iced tea."

"Grape."

Tiki was just pouring out their drinks when Ronde said, "Hey, what was that about, after I ran back that kick-off for the TD?"

"What was what about?"

"You said 'That's it!' or something like that."

"Oh, yeah." Tiki grinned. "You gave me the answer to the hardest question this week."

"You mean for your column?"

"Actually, this one's not going into the column, but I've been thinking on it all week."

"What was it?"

"I can't talk about it."

"Huh? Why not?"

"Sworn to secrecy."

Ronde frowned. He didn't like it when they had secrets from each other. Neither did Tiki, but in this case he couldn't help it. Cootie had begged him not to tell anyone, especially Ronde.

"About that column of yours," Ronde said, zoning in on Tiki as he checked the oven. "What's up with it?"

"What do you mean, what's up with it?" Tiki asked.

"How long are you gonna be doing it? I mean, I've got to be honest, your game is suffering, and your grades aren't doing too good either."

"I know it," Tiki said. "Thing is, I like doing it. Kids

look up to you, you know? They respect you for something besides being a good athlete."

"People respect you for that anyway," Ronde pointed out. Neither of them was touching their food. This conversation had suddenly turned deadly serious. "You get good grades, you're a good friend, a good person, you're funny—not as funny as me, but funny. Man, you've got a lot going for you. You don't need to be a guidance counselor for free."

Tiki sighed. "I hear what you're saying," he said. "But I promised Laura I'd do the column. It's not that easy to back out. You know how she is, and I promised I would."

"Talk to her, dude. I'm sure she's an Eagles fan. She wouldn't want us to go down in flames. Tell her it's just too much for you. After all, it's the truth, isn't it?" He paused, waiting for Tiki to reply. "Isn't it?" he repeated, staring his brother down.

"You're right, man. I know you're right," Tiki admitted. "But I can't back out just like that."

"You've got to do it, and fast," Ronde said. "Kids on the team are already grumbling about it behind your back."

"Which kids?" Tiki demanded.

"Can't tell," Ronde said. "Sworn to secrecy."

Tiki frowned. Ronde had him, and he knew it. "Tell you what," Tiki said, "I'll write one last column, and that's it. I'll beg off . . . for the rest of the football season. I'll tell Laura I can start the column again after that."

"There, you see? That's a good solution!" Ronde said, breaking into a smile. "Man, you're not as dumb as you look."

"I'll do it, on one condition," Tiki said, breaking into a sly grin himself.

"Condition? What condition?"

"That you agree to write the column with me." Tiki sat back and folded his hands on his chest. "There. That's my offer. Take it or leave it."

"Nuh-uh, no way!" Ronde said, pounding the table. "Who said you got to set conditions?"

"I say. Now, what do you say?"

"I say no. Didn't you hear me the first time?"

"Okay, then," Tiki said, grabbing his fork and spearing some mac and cheese with it. "I guess I'll just keep writing the column, then."

"Tiki, think of the team!"

"YOU think of the team," Tiki said. "If you want us to win, just agree to write the column with me."

"That's blackmail!"

"Come on, Ronde," Tiki said, softening. "You know you're the one who always has the best advice for people. Remember Cody last week? I'm telling you, dude, you're a natural!"

"I'm not that good at writing," Ronde said, hesitating.

"I can help you get better at it," Tiki offered. "Hey, I won the essay prize. What better writing coach could you want?"

"I don't know . . ."

"Don't you want to be a better writer?"

"Tiki!"

"Don't you want to help kids solve their problems?"

"Come on . . ."

"Don't you want to have something else you're good at, in case we don't make the NFL someday?"

"Now, that's going too far," Ronde said. "We *are* making the NFL. *Both* of us. No doubts allowed."

"Fine, fine. Just agree to do the column with me. Please? It'll be fun. You'll see. Twice as easy with two of us doing it, and twice as fun." He held out his hand for Ronde to shake.

Ronde frowned. "You owe me for this, big-time," he said, taking Tiki's hand and sealing the deal with their private handshake.

"You won't be sorry, Ronde," Tiki said.

"I'm already sorry."

"Now," Tiki said, not listening anymore, "how am I going to answer this student . . . ?"

Dear Cootie,

I've been thinking and thinking about your problem, and here's my best advice: Just be yourself, and be proud of

who you are. That's what it all comes down to. Here's
what I mean.

My brother is smaller than I am, but he always says
"Good things come in small packages." Yesterday he
made a big play in the game *because* he was so small.
"They never saw me coming," he told me afterward.
And that made me think of you, Cootie.

Don't let them see you coming. They're expecting you
to get upset, to cry, to run away when they bully you.
Don't give them what they're expecting. Keep them
off balance. Laugh at yourself along with them! Or say
something they don't understand, something that makes
them scratch their heads and think, "What did he mean
by that?"

Don't get down in the gutter with them either. Show
them you're made of better stuff than that, and that you
won't sink to their level. Don't talk trash about them
behind their backs, because sooner or later they'll find
out and they'll know you were upset by their bullying,
which is just what they want. So don't give it to them.

It's not everyone who's brave enough not to care what
people think or say about them. It's not everyone who's
brave enough to wear a full-body eagle suit and dance
around in front of hundreds of people. It's not everyone
who's brave enough to show their passion for their
favorite team the way you do.

You're brave, Cootie. So show them that. Show them
all. Sooner or later they'll feel ashamed for making fun
of such a brave kid, and they'll quit doing it. That's my
advice, for what it's worth.

Play proud.

Your friend,
Tiki.

Tiki put the letter in an envelope, put Cootie's name on the front of it, and tucked it into his book bag. There. That was one letter out of the way. Tiki turned to the other letters. "Okay, who's next?" he said aloud, reaching for the pile.

"What do you mean, your final column? You're quitting?" Laura blinked at him rapidly in disbelief. "But it's the most successful feature we've had in years! You can't quit now!"

"Sorry," Tiki told her. "My grades are suffering, the team is suffering, and I'm suffering. I never thought there'd be this many letters to answer."

"Just answer one per week, and forget the rest!" Laura offered, sounding desperate.

"Nuh-uh," said Tiki. "Those kids deserve an answer just as much. It's not easy to reveal your problems to somebody in writing. I don't want to leave them all hanging. But don't worry. I'll start the column again after football season, and I'll have Ronde doing it with me."

"Ronde?"

"You can call it 'Dear Twins' or something like that."

"Hmmm. Not bad," she said, cocking her head to one

side and considering the idea from all angles. "Okay, that's fine. But what about this week?"

"Here's the letter to publish," he said, handing it to her. "And here are the others, for the pickup box." He gave her the other letters. The one for Cootie was still in his bag. He'd give it to Cootie later, at practice. He was always there, bringing water and sports drinks and towels to the players.

"Cool. Oh, and I'll need a farewell letter," she said. "I'm not going to be the one who has to explain this to the student body."

"Got it," said Tiki, giving it to her.

She opened the note and read it. "Dear Students, I want to thank you for your support these last few weeks. Unfortunately, I will be taking a break from this column, starting next week, until the end of football season. I'm sure you understand that I want to give all my attention to the team. It's my last season here, and I want us to repeat as state champs. That plus schoolwork made doing the column and answering all your wonderful letters just too much for me to handle. However, when I come back, I'll have help. My twin brother, Ronde, the best advice-giver in our family except for my mom, will be joining me and writing the answers alongside me. I hope you'll support him the same way you have me. Thank you, and see you again in the spring semester. Your friend and adviser, Tiki Barber."

She looked up and him. "Not bad," she said, cracking a smile. "Who knew you could write?"

"Thanks, Laura," he said, relieved. "Thanks for understanding. I know I promised you, but—"

"Oh, yeah, right," she said. "Like I took that seriously. I knew you agreed just to get out of answering Suzie on the spot. You think I'm blind?"

"You knew that? And you still made me keep my promise?"

She shrugged and grinned at him. "Hey," she said. "A girl's gotta do what a girl's gotta do. The paper needed a boost, and I went out and got the biggest star in the school to work for us. Two points for me." She gave him a quick punch in the shoulder. "See you around," she said. "And come spring, I've got a commitment from both of you, right?"

"Right," Tiki assured her, rubbing where she'd hit him. Man, that girl sure could throw a right hook!

The Jefferson game was a revelation. The Panthers had been a losing team last season, and this year was no different. Their offense was inexperienced, and their defense was weak. They had no answer for Tiki Barber— not this new Tiki, who was running with a focus and determination his fellow Eagles had never seen before.

By halftime he'd run for three touchdowns and more than a hundred yards. In the second half he was even better, scoring three more times, twice with runs of more than fifty yards. By the time the game was over (the outcome had been inevitable since the first quarter), the Eagles had a 54–14 victory and were looking like the juggernaut everyone thought they would be.

No more bumbling, fumbling first halves. No more furious, desperate second-half comebacks. This was a massacre of the first order, and Tiki was looking like the beast of the league, a player who could take the heart out of a defense.

"We're gonna do it, Ronde," he told his brother after the game. "We're gonna go undefeated this year."

"You guaranteeing it?"

"No, man. I'm not that stupid. It's early yet. Anything could happen. Think of last year."

Ronde nodded, and whistled. Last year had been a series of cliff-hangers, a roller-coaster ride filled with tension and flirting with disaster.

This year, now that they'd gotten over the hump, was looking like much smoother sailing.

"It does look good, doesn't it?" Ronde agreed. As he said the word "does," his voice cracked, as it had lately begun to do.

"Uh-oh," said Tiki. "There you go."

"There I go what?"

"Your voice cracked, dude."

"Did not."

"Did too. Hey, don't fight it. Mine's been cracking for

months. It means you're hitting your growth spurt!"

"It does?"

"Yeah, man. You'll see. You'll start growing like a bean stalk any day now."

Ronde nodded, picturing it. "Yeah," he said. "Maybe I should try to make it crack some more."

Tiki shook his head. "Don't bother. It'll just happen," he assured his twin. "You'll see. Good things come to those who wait."

"Hey!" Ronde said. "That's another famous saying!"

"Is it?" Tiki said, grinning. "And here I thought I made it up."

# FOOTBALL TERMS

## CUTBACK:

A running play where the ballcarrier runs in one direction and then suddenly changes direction to advance the ball past the line of scrimmage.

## DRAW:

A play where the quarterback goes back as if to pass and then hands off to the running back.

## DROP KICK:

A play where the kicker first drops the ball on the ground and then kicks it for an extra point or a punt.

## END-AROUND:

A running play where the ballcarrier runs around the end of the defensive line for positive yardage.

## HALFBACK OPTION PLAY:

A passing play where the quarterback hands off or laterals the ball to the halfback who throws the pass.

## LATERAL PASS:

A pass where the quarterback or ballcarrier tosses the ball behind them to another runner who can then advance the ball.

## OFF-TACKLE RUN:

A running play where the ballcarrier runs behind the tackle.

## QUARTERBACK OPTION RUN:

A running play where the quarterback runs right or left with either the fullback or halfback following and then the quarterback has the option of continuing to run or making a lateral pass to the following back.

## QUARTERBACK SNEAK:

A running play where the quarterback takes a step back as if to pass and then runs the ball up the middle.

### REVERSE:

A pass play where the quarterback hands off the ball to a runner who is running around the end and then another ball handler comes around in the opposite direction and is handed the ball.

### SAFETY BLITZ:

A play where one or more linebackers cross the line of scrimmage to tackle the quarterback.

### SCREEN PASS:

A pass play where the defense rushes the quarterback and then the quarterback throws over the onrushing line to a back or receiver.

### SLANT:

A pass play where the wide receiver runs his route diagonally across the field.

# ABOUT THE AUTHORS

**TIKI BARBER** grew up in Roanoke, Virginia, where he wore number 2 for the Cave Spring Eagles during junior high school. From 1997 through 2006 he wore number 21 as a running back for the New York Giants, where he holds every rushing record in team history, and was a three-time Pro Bowl selection.

**RONDE BARBER** wore number 5 for the Cave Spring Eagles. Today he is one of the top cornerbacks in the NFL and wears number 20 for the Tampa Bay Buccaneers. Ronde is a Super Bowl winner, a five-time Pro Bowl selection, and the first cornerback in the history of the league to have at least twenty-five sacks and forty interceptions in a career.

**TIKI and RONDE BARBER** have collaborated on seven children's books, *By My Brother's Side*, the Christopher Award–winning *Game Day*, *Teammates*, *Kickoff!*, *Go Long!*, *Wild Card*, and most recently, *Red Zone*.

**PAUL MANTELL** is the author of more than one hundred books for young readers.